★ MAVERICKS

Welcome to Montana—the home of bold men
and daring women, where more than fifty tales
of passion, adventure and intrigue unfold
beneath the Big Sky. Don't miss a single one!

Montana ★ MAVERICKS

CHRISTINE RIMMER

Cinderella's Big Sky Groom

Silhouette® Books

Published by Silhouette Books

America's Publisher of Contemporary Romance

Special thanks and acknowledgment to Christine Rimmer
for her contribution to the Montana Mavericks series.

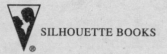 SILHOUETTE BOOKS

Recycling programs
for this product may
not exist in your area.

ISBN-13: 978-0-373-31039-5
ISBN-10:   0-373-31039-0

CINDERELLA'S BIG SKY GROOM

Copyright © 1999 by Harlequin Books S.A.

Visit Silhouette Books at www.eHarlequin.com

Printed in U.S.A.

CHRISTINE RIMMER

came to her profession the long way around. Before settling down to write about the magic of romance, she'd been an actress, a salesclerk, a janitor, a model, a phone sales representative, a teacher, a waitress, a playwright and an office manager. Now that she's finally found work that suits her perfectly, she insists she never had a problem keeping a job—she was merely gaining "life experience" for her future as a novelist. Those who know her best withhold comment when she makes such claims; they are grateful that she's at last found steady work. Christine is grateful, too—not only for the joy she finds in writing, but for what waits when the day's work is through: a man she loves who loves her right back, and the privilege of watching their children grow and change day to day. She lives with her family in Oklahoma.

For Betty Lowe, a dear friend and dedicated reader.
This one's just for you, Betty.

Chapter One

Lynn Taylor set down her pencil. "Sara?"

The child, the only one of Lynn's kindergartners who hadn't left for the day, lifted her shining blond head from the picture she'd been working on.

"What time is it?" Lynn asked.

Sara turned to look at the clock on the wall above the chalkboard. "Little hand on the twelve. Big hand on the two...." Her expression turned grave as she processed that information. After a moment she ventured cautiously, "Ten minutes after twelve?"

"That's right."

A sunny smile burst forth. "That means my mommy's coming real soon to take you for your birthday surprise."

"Yes, she is. And I think you'd better—"

"It's a *big* surprise, Miss Taylor."

"I know. Your mother told me. And so did you. Several times."

"And I can't tell you *anything* more."

"You told me that, too."

"Because Mommy said you have to wait. That's what it means, when you get a surprise. You wait and wait."

"Yes, and I think you'd better—"

"It's like at Christmas, when you have a *big* present and it's under the tree and your mommy won't let you even tear off just a little bit of the pretty paper to see what's in there. And every morning you get up and you look at it and you know you can't open it till Christmas. And that kind of makes you a little bit mad, because you want to know what it is so bad. But you are *etcited,* too, because you know it's something real special in there, maybe a great big doll or…everything for a puppy that would grow up to be just like Jenny's dog, Sugar."

"Sara—"

"You know, I mean, your mommy couldn't put a puppy in a box for all that time, so it would just be the puppy bed and some puppy food and bones for him to chew on. And your mommy would be keeping the puppy someplace safe so that, when Christmas morning came, you could—"

"Sara."

The child caught herself—finally. "Uh. Yes, Miss Taylor?"

Lynn mimed pulling a zipper across her lips.

"Oh. Okay."

"I think it's time you put your picture away and got ready to go."

"Yes, Miss Taylor…but you know what?"

"What?"

"I really hope I get a puppy someday."

"And maybe you will. But right now—"

"I know." She giggled. "Zipper my lip."

"That's right."

Holding her drawing in one hand, Sara flipped up her desktop with the other—then peeked around the top at Lynn. "And put my coat on."

"Yes." Lynn closed her lesson plan book and stuck it in her top desk drawer as Sara tucked her drawing away, shut her desk and pushed her chair back.

Right then, there were three strong taps on the door that led to the outside hall. Sara chirped out, "I'll get it! It's probably Mommy...." She shoved her chair into place under the desk and darted for the door, grasping the steel knob and giving it a hearty push.

The door swung outward on its hydraulic hinge and a chilly gust of October wind blew in, ruffling the loose papers on Lynn's desk. Lynn saw them start to fly. With a low laugh, she put her hand over the stack. "Come on in and close that—"

"It's not my mommy," said Sara. "It's a *man*."

Lynn looked up—and right into a pair of dark, uncompromising eyes.

Her gaze moved down, over strong cheekbones and a well-shaped nose. Along a square jaw and a chin possessed of an absolutely perfect masculine cleft. His clothing—a chocolate-brown sport coat, dark slacks and tooled boots—spoke quietly of money. Lynn knew who he was. Ross Garrison. Whitehorn's new lawyer. Lynn had never actually met him, but she'd seen him around town. And her younger stepsister, Trish, was his secretary. Since Trish lived with Lynn, Lynn had heard all about him, in gushing, adoring detail.

Another gust of wind blew in. Lynn shivered. And found her voice. "Mr. Garrison, isn't it?"

"Yes."

"Well, please. Come in. And let Sara close the door."

He stepped into the classroom. Sara pulled the door shut. Lynn took her hand off the stack of papers and stood. Resisting the urge to smooth out her plain wool skirt, she moved around from behind the desk.

"I'm looking for Lynn Taylor," the lawyer announced. "The woman at the office said—"

"You have the right room. I'm Lynn."

He extended a large, tanned, beautifully shaped hand. At first she thought he wanted to shake. But no. He was holding a business card. She took it.

As the card changed hands, his gaze ran over her in a cursory fashion—and then went straight on by.

Lynn glanced down at the card. It was cream colored, of thick, linenlike stock, rich and rough textured under the pad of her thumb. His name was in gold ink: Ross Garrison, Attorney-at-Law. In smaller black print, in the lower left-hand corner, she saw the address and phone number of his law office on Center Street.

She looked up at him once more. He was still gazing past her—and scanning her classroom, as if inspecting it for flaws. Those dark, knowing eyes took in the chalkboards and the wall displays of alphabets and brightly colored numbers.

"An attractive setup," he said.

"Thank you." She waited for him to say why he'd come.

But he didn't. Instead, he began prowling her room, scrutinizing the October calendar, with its border of black cats, witches' hats and autumn leaves. He paused at the student storyboard, where the little booklets her students had made with such care and bound with bright yarn dangled from pushpins. Finally he stopped by the far wall, opposite her, and stared out over the study-group arrangement of the desks.

"Yes," he said, rather officiously. "This is very good."

Lynn turned to Sara, who was standing—silent for once, and rather wide-eyed—by the door. "Go on into the coat nook, honey, and put on that jacket. Get your pack, too. Make sure you've got your snack box and your art supplies. Your mom should be here any minute."

Obediently, Sara trotted off toward the small anteroom, where the children hung up their coats and stored their personal belongings in individual cubbies.

Once Sara was gone, Lynn asked cautiously, "Is this...something about Trish?"

The lawyer left off examining her room and deigned to look at her again. There was nothing in his eyes. Not even a glimmer of interest at the mention of her sister's name. This was somewhat bothersome to Lynn, as she knew that Trish had big plans for the man. Plans that included a white gown, a veil with a long train and a walk down the aisle of the Whitehorn Community Church.

"No," he said. "This has nothing to do with my secretary. She's your stepsister, isn't she?"

Lynn gave him a tight, careful smile. "I can see you've done your homework."

He shrugged. "Your sister likes to talk. I've heard all about you." More, she guessed from his tone, than he'd wanted to know. "I've also heard a lot about your other stepsister, Arlene, and Arlene's husband and their children. *And* about your stepmother. I believe her name is Jewel." He looked weary. Trish's prospects for marriage with this man looked dimmer by the second.

In fact, judging by his tone and his expression, Lynn couldn't help wondering how long her sister would have her job. Trish wasn't much of a typist. And if she talked about her personal life when she should have been working, her future with Ross Garrison, Attorney-at-Law, did not look especially secure.

Lynn suppressed a sigh. "Well, if you're not here about my sister, then why *are* you here?"

He moved a few steps, until he was standing beside her desk. He looked down at the desk blotter, at the stack of In boxes in the corner, at the pen stand, which was shaped like a shiny red apple.

Feeling a need to protect her own space from his prying eyes, Lynn moved to the other side of the desk and confronted him across it. "Mr. Garrison?"

He looked up again. "Hmm? Oh." And the corners of his mouth lifted. It was a stunning smile. Easy and casual. Charming and a little rueful. "Sorry. Lawyer's habit. Observation."

Lynn did not smile back. She considered herself a patient, forgiving soul as a rule, but she'd had about enough of this man looking over her room as if he owned it, and not answering her when she asked what he wanted. "Why are you here?"

He cleared his throat. "I've come about Jennifer McCallum."

Jenny, Lynn thought, feeling more wary—and more protective—by the second. Jenny had been through more trouble and tragedy in her five short years than some endured in a lifetime. Lynn had a definite soft spot for the child, as did almost everyone in Whitehorn.

"I'm the new attorney for the girl's estate," Ross Garrison said. "And I've also been named a trustee."

"You're taking Wendell Hargrove's place?" She allowed her disapproval to come through in her tone.

One dark eyebrow inched upward. "I intend to do a better job than Hargrove did, I promise you."

"I should hope so." Wendell Hargrove had once been greatly respected in Whitehorn. For a number of years he'd represented the Kincaid estate, to which little Jenny was now the primary heir. In the end, though, he'd stolen from the clients he was supposed to be representing, including Jenny. He was serving time in prison now.

Ross Garrison glanced down. The stack of In boxes was right by his hand. Idly, he ran a finger along the rim of the top box. His watch caught the overhead light and gleamed dully. Silver? No. Platinum. The man actually owned a platinum watch.

Whitehorn, Montana, wasn't exactly the sleepy cow town it had once been. But platinum watches were still few and far between in those parts.

The lawyer looked up again and into Lynn's eyes.

"I'm just doing my job, Miss Taylor. Working up Jennifer McCallum's file. With an estate of this size, it's important that I cover all the bases, get a firm grip on what I'm dealing with here, for the good of my client. In future, decisions will have to be made concerning investments. And also concerning possible changes in the terms of the trust. I want to be sure I approach those decisions with my eyes open. I want, sincerely, to do the best I can by Jennifer. I've interviewed her doctor and her adoptive parents in depth and—"

"Now it's time to talk to her teacher."

"Exactly."

They regarded each other across the width of the desk. It was the strangest moment. Perhaps because there seemed to be so much unexplainable tension in it. Or maybe because, for the first time, Lynn felt he was actually looking at her. Closely. Probingly...

"Jenny? You want to know about Jenny?"

Lynn turned at the sound of Sara's voice. The child stood in the entrance to the coat nook. She had on her red jacket, and clutched her dark blue pack, partially unzipped and hanging open. Inside, Lynn spotted the edge of a hot-pink art supply box—which she knew belonged to Jenny McCallum. Those two were forever trading things. Lynn would bet a gross of number-two pencils that Sara's neon-yellow art box had gone home in Jenny's pack.

"That's right, Sara," Ross Garrison said. Lynn had to give him credit. She'd said Sara's name only once—*Let Sara close the door*—and he had remembered it. "I'm here to learn all I can about Jenny McCallum." He smiled that too-charming smile of his.

His smile and the sound of her name were all the encouragement Sara needed.

"Jenny is my best friend in the whole, wide world," she announced. "She's smart and she has blue eyes and blond hair, just like me. We look like sisters. Everybody says so. And we really like that, because we both wish we had a sister—or even a brother. But we don't. But Jenny does have a dog. Her name is Sugar. And I want a dog. I really do. A puppy all for my own. And tomorrow night I'm going to Jenny's house to have a sleepover. Her mom said we might even go out to the ranch—the *Kincaid* ranch. We might get to pet the barn cats and feed the horses some apples and—"

"Sara." Lynn pantomimed zipping up her mouth.

Sara got the message. She pressed her cute pink lips together—but then the outside door swung open again and she crowed, "There you are, Mommy!"

Danielle Mitchell slid inside and shut the door. Grinning, she sketched a bow at Lynn. "Your fairy godmother has arrived...and what's this? Legal troubles?"

"Mrs. Mitchell, how are you?"

"Just fine. And didn't I tell you to call me Danielle?"

"Yes, you certainly did."

Lynn glanced from her friend to the lawyer. She hadn't realized they knew each other. But then again, this *was* Whitehorn. Everybody knew everybody. It had always been that way.

"So what's up?" Danielle demanded of Lynn.

Garrison answered for her. "Just gathering information. I've been hired to represent the Kincaid estate, and that means Jennifer McCallum is now one of my clients.''

''You're here to interview Lynn about Jenny?''

''That's right.''

''And there's not much to say,'' Lynn put in firmly. ''Jennifer is doing just fine. She is happy, intelligent, outgoing and unstintingly adored by one and all.''

Garrison gave her the raised eyebrow again. *''Unstintingly?''*

Lynn felt…irritated, that was it. Irritated by this too-good-looking big-city lawyer, who had waltzed into her classroom, looked around as if he owned the place, acted bored to death at the mention of her sister—who might be a bit flighty, but nonetheless had stars in her eyes when it came to him—and then began giving *her* the third degree about Jenny. ''Yes. That's what I said. Jenny is unstintingly adored by everyone.''

''My, my,'' Danielle muttered under her breath. ''Feeling feisty today, aren't we?''

Lynn shot her friend a quelling glance, then turned on Garrison again. ''She's a lovely child. And one of my two best students—Sara here is the other one.'' She glanced at Sara, who granted her a big, proud smile.

Ross Garrison was not smiling. ''Miss Taylor. We both know that Jennifer's been through considerable trauma.''

''Yes. She has. And in my opinion, none of her troubles have damaged her in the least.''

Garrison did not look convinced, but he did allow, ''Fine. If you say so.''

''I do.''

"All right."

"Good."

Those dark eyes stared into hers again, taking her measure. Lynn stared right back at him. Finally he said, "Listen, I really would like to talk with you in a little more depth about this."

Danielle chuckled then. "You'll have to wait your turn, Ross. Lynn's going to be busy for a while. But you could meet her at the Whitehorn Beauty Salon— say, about five?"

Lynn blinked and whirled on her friend. "The Whitehorn Salon? Wait a minute. You didn't say anything about taking me there."

Danielle looked way too pleased with herself. "It was a surprise, remember?"

"But…" Lynn couldn't help sputtering. "But… the *beauty shop?* For *five hours?*"

Danielle waved a hand. "Four and a half, actually. Your appointment's at twelve-thirty." She glanced at the clock. "And we'd better get going or we'll be late."

"But Danielle—"

The other woman cut her off by speaking to Garrison. "Like I said. Whitehorn Salon. Five o'clock. She'll be there."

Lynn sputtered some more. "No. No, wait, I—"

"Five o'clock, then," said Ross Garrison. And before Lynn could finish objecting, he strode to the door, pushed it open and left in a swirl of brisk autumn air.

Chapter Two

The moment the door closed behind the lawyer, Lynn demanded of her friend, "Why did you tell him where to find me?"

"Why not? He just wants to get up to speed about Jenny."

"Well, I know, but..."

"But what?" There was a very suspicious gleam in Danielle's eyes. "Are you *scared* of him, or something?"

"Of course not."

"Well, I have to say, sparks certainly seemed to be flying between you two."

"They were not. Not in the least. A man like that is never going to look twice at someone like me."

"There you go. Underestimating yourself again."

"I am not. I'm just stating a fact. And I'm not looking twice at him, either. He's—" She cut herself off as she realized that Sara was standing right there, taking all this in. "Never mind. I just...well, I told him all there is to tell. You heard me."

"Oh, come on. Let him do his job. He seems... very conscientious. And after Wendell Hargrove, Jenny deserves a lawyer who's looking out for her interests instead of robbing her blind."

Sara was still staring up at them. "Mommy. Jenny's not blind. She can see just fine."

Danielle smoothed her daughter's unruly bangs back from her forehead. "It's just an expression, honey. Jenny had a bad lawyer who took some of her money. But now that bad lawyer's gone to jail."

"And that man who just left, he's a lawyer, too?"

"That's right. He's Jenny's new lawyer."

"Is he *good* lawyer?"

"Yes. I'm sure he is."

"What's a lawyer, anyway? And how come, if Jenny's got one, I don't?"

Danielle glanced at the clock. "We'll have to talk about that later. Right now, we need to get going."

To the Whitehorn Salon, Lynn thought with a considerable degree of dread. "Danielle, I don't know about this..."

"I do. Did you bring the red dress?"

"Danielle. I really don't think—"

"Come on. Just answer me. Did you bring the dress?"

Lynn was a little embarrassed about that dress. She'd bought it on a shopping trip to Billings just two weeks before, a shopping trip where she'd intended only to replace a few of the practical skirts and blouses that were now three sizes too large. She hadn't *meant* to buy a dress like that. It had cost too much and it wasn't the kind of thing she'd ever actually wear, anyway.

"Lynn. The dress? Did you bring it?"

"Yes. I brought it."

"And those red shoes, too?"

Lynn huffed out a breath. The shoes had two-inch heels. Lynn was five-nine in stocking feet. She always wore flats. What in the world had possessed her to buy a pair shoes that would only make her look even taller?

"The shoes, Lynn?" Danielle asked for the second time with clearly diminishing patience.

"Yes, all right, I brought the shoes, too."

"Good. Get 'em and let's go. You can ride with me and Sara."

"I can take my own—"

Danielle grunted. "No way. You've got that rabbity look around the eyes. You might just drive on home instead of where I'm taking you."

"Danielle…"

"Stop arguing. You're coming with us and you can pick up your Blazer later."

"But Danielle. To the *beauty salon?*"

"Yes. To the beauty salon. You've lost, what? Twenty-five pounds?"

"Twenty-eight."

"You should be proud of yourself."

"I *am* proud of myself."

"Good. Because you look great. And for your birthday, I intend to make sure we put the finishing touches on your transformation."

"I just don't know about this."

"Get that dress and those shoes and let's go."

* * *

Lynn was still trying to protest when Danielle pushed her into the padded stylist's chair and the salon's owner, Gracie Donahue, whisked a big purple hairdresser's cape around her neck.

"I can't believe I'm doing this. This is all just too much...."

"It is not," said Gracie's daughter, Kim, with whom Lynn had gone to school—and who was now in town on a visit from San Francisco, where she worked in a very exclusive salon. "I'm in on this, too. And I am the best at what I do. You're going to look fabulous when we're through. All the cowboys for miles around will fall in love with you."

Lynn stared at her own reflection in the mirror. No one to fall in love with there. True, her clean-scrubbed face was slimmer than it used to be. She actually had cheekbones now. But she still looked as ordinary as a loaf of white bread. Also, right at the moment, her brow was furrowed and her mouth all pinched up. "Oh, I don't like this...." It came out on a whimper.

Kim laughed. "Wait till we're finished. First, a deep-pore cleansing. Then the mud mask. Manicure. And pedicure. The hair, of course—and full makeup, once your pores have had a chance to settle down from the cleansing and the mask."

That didn't sound particularly comforting. "My pores have to *settle down?*"

"Yes. And they will. We have plenty of time. You'll walk out of here a new woman."

"I'm just fine the way I am." She wished she sounded more convincing.

"Of course you are. But there's always room for improvement."

"It's too much...."

Kim gave a delicate snort. "You already said that."

Lynn caught Danielle's eye in the mirror. "You know you can't afford all this." Danielle was a single mom on a limited budget. "It will be far too expensive."

Gracie put her plump hands on Lynn's shoulders. "Listen." Lynn stiffened. Gracie's warm fingers pressed a little more firmly. "I mean it."

Sara piped up then. "Miss Taylor, you have to sit still if you want to get your surprise. You have to let them make you beautiful, just like Cinderella. Remember? When her fairy godmother came and got out her magic wand and sang the 'Bibbidi-Bobbidi-Boo' song and Cinderella's hair got so pretty and her raggedy dress turned into a magic ball gown and the little mouses turned into horses and the big pumpkin turned into—"

"Honey." Danielle shook her head.

Sara put her hand over her mouth. "Oops."

Gracie said, "There are some coloring books in the cabinet under the table in the waiting area. Maybe Sara would have some fun with them?"

"Coloring books?" Sara asked with interest.

Danielle shot her friend a reassuring smile. "Relax." Then she took her daughter's hand. "Let's go check them out."

Danielle led her daughter away and Gracie faced Lynn in the mirror once more. "Now. Are you listening?"

"Yes, but—"

"Hush. Are you listening?"

Lynn gulped and nodded.

Gracie said, "I've lived in Whitehorn all my life."

"Well, Gracie, I know that."

"And *I* went to school with you," Kim added.

Lynn felt defensive. "What are you getting at?"

"The truth," said Gracie. "That's what you get from your hairdresser, if you're lucky. A decent cut and a little honesty. We've all watched you over the years, so quiet and unassuming and sweet, letting that Jewel and her two spoiled darlings run right over you."

Lynn's defensiveness increased. "Please don't speak ill of my family."

Gracie tightened her grip on Lynn's shoulders again. "I'm not speaking ill of them. I'm only speaking the truth. I know you love them. And I'm sure they love you. In their own selfish ways. And that's great. That's fine. But the truth is, you've never allowed yourself to shine, now, have you?"

"I don't really see how—"

"How much weight have you lost in the past six months?" Grace demanded.

Lynn gulped again. "It really hasn't been in the past six months. It's been longer." Since her father had died two years before, actually. Because she'd been so sad, and not felt much like eating. And then later, as her grief had faded, the calorie-laden junk foods she had once craved no longer held such strong appeal. "It's just…taken everyone a while to notice, I guess."

"Well, however long it's taken, you are lookin' good. And after today, you're going to look even better. And you don't have to worry about Danielle's pocketbook, because Kimmy and I are going in on this birthday present, too. Understand?"

"But—"

"*Understand?*"

Lynn gulped again.

Gracie and Kim looked at her sternly.

And then, in the mirror, she watched a smile tremble across her own mouth.

Why, she thought, I *want* this. I truly do. I'm *ready* for this. It's my twenty-fourth birthday, and Gracie Donahue is right. It's about time I let myself shine.

Danielle appeared in the mirror again, on Gracie's right side. Lynn looked from Kim to Gracie—and to her friend last of all. Danielle winked at her.

Lynn sucked in a long breath. "Okay. Wave that magic wand."

Gracie squeezed her shoulders one more time and then let go.

"And thank you."

The three behind her chair chorused, "You're welcome," in unison.

"And…well, I'm still pretty nervous."

"It's all right," said Gracie. "Be nervous. But stay put until we're done with you."

It took over an hour just for the facial. Then they started on her hair: a foil wrap first. Then they did her nails, both manicure *and* pedicure, as promised. Several other customers came in during the process. Lynn knew most of them. They smiled and greeted her, and didn't seem at all surprised that plain Lynn Taylor had suddenly decided to spend a whole afternoon being primped and pampered.

Lynn had a nice little nap under her mud mask. And then she sat under the dryer with the coloring goo and bits of foil stuck in her hair and read a magazine from front to back. She went to the back room briefly, to remove her panty hose, then stretched out in the stylist's chair while Gracie filed and painted her nails, top and bottom. Once her nails were dry, she made another quick trip to the back room, to put her stockings and her shoes on again.

When she emerged, Gracie led her to the chair once more. Lynn settled in with a contented sigh, wondering why she'd never given herself permission to do this before. Even if the makeover didn't "take," she thought with a secret smile, she might do this again just for the sheer relaxing enjoyment of having other women tend to her. It was so soothing, so leisurely, lying there with her eyes closed, hearing their laughter as they talked and joked about their jobs and their men, as they discussed their children and their dreams for them. The gentle, firm touch of skillful hands took all her cares away as they massaged in the mud mask, twisted her hair into the bits of foil—and later, rubbed shampoo into her scalp, then fluttered around her head, snipping away at the freshly highlighted strands.

Finally Kim turned her so that she couldn't see the mirror. "Don't look again until I'm finished."

Kim went to work with a blow dryer and a styling brush. When Lynn's hair was styled to her satisfaction, she slid an elastic band around Lynn's head, to keep the hair out of the way. Then, with light, deft strokes, she applied the makeup that Gracie and Danielle, hovering near, declared brought out those newly discovered cheekbones of hers and made her lashes seem longer, her eyes a much deeper blue.

Even little Sara had been allowed to come near again by then. "You look so *beautiful,* Miss Taylor," she said, sighing. "Just like I said. Like Cinderella. All you need is your ball gown and your glass slippers. And your prince. You're really going to need a prince. He can take you to the ball and you can dance until midnight—when *both* hands are on the twelve. And then, when midnight comes and your horses are just about ready to turn into mouses again, you can run down the palace steps so fast that one of your glass slippers will fall off and the prince will have a way to find you later, when—"

"Sara," said Danielle tenderly. She gave her daughter the zip-up-your-lip signal and the child subsided.

Finally Kim took the headband away and removed the hairdresser's cape. She brushed Lynn's hair back into place, spritzed on a light mist of holding spray. Then she dabbed perfume along the curve of her neck and at each wrist.

"What is that?" Lynn asked, sniffing.

"Poison."

"*What?*"

Kim chuckled. "This perfume is called Poison. Deadly name, killer scent."

Lynn sniffed again. "It *is* nice."

"Would I steer you wrong?"

"Don't look yet," Danielle commanded when Kim set the amethyst-colored bottle of scent aside.

Kim showed Lynn a diagram—a drawing of a woman's face, marked in the places where foundation, blusher, eye and lip color should be applied. She also offered a small box of makeup samples. "These are the products I think you should use. I've done you for evening. For daytime, just tone down the blusher, go light on foundation and skip the shimmery eye shadow. Go with that subtle blue-gray.''

Lynn murmured her thanks and tried to turn toward the mirror.

Danielle grabbed the arm of the chair. ''Not yet.'' She held out Lynn's brown shoulder bag. ''Put that stuff away first, so you won't forget it.''

So Lynn put the diagram and the box of samples into her purse. ''*Now* may I see?''

''Soon.'' Danielle produced a red scarf.

Lynn raised a skeptical eyebrow at that scarf. ''This is getting very silly.''

''Indulge us.'' Danielle tied the scarf over Lynn's eyes—carefully, in order not to muss her makeup or her hair. ''Now come on. Give me your hand.''

Lynn felt Danielle's fingers close around hers.

''Step clear of the footrest,'' Danielle instructed. ''Good. Now, come this way....''

Lynn knew where Danielle was leading her—to the small back room, where her red dress and red shoes were waiting. She followed obediently, trusting the clasp of her friend's soft hand.

When they reached their destination, Danielle said, ''Wait right here.'' She released Lynn's hand. Lynn heard the door close. Then Danielle returned to her. She helped Lynn remove her cardigan sweater, her blouse and her wool skirt.

''I'm feeling really pampered about now,'' Lynn said as Danielle pulled the kitten-soft cashmere sweater dress over her head.

Danielle gave a low, musical laugh. ''That's the point.''

''I'm sure glad you came to Whitehorn.''

''I kind of like the place myself.''

Danielle had moved to town two years before, right around the time Lynn's father had died. Lynn had met her at the Whitehorn library, where Danielle had found a twenty-hour-a-week job right away. They'd liked each other on sight. The friendship had just seemed to happen, so naturally.

And they'd grown even closer the past two months, with Sara in Lynn's class and Danielle taking on the job of Room Mom. Danielle often came in during class time to help out with special projects. She also tended to linger after school when she came to pick up Sara, helping Lynn with her room displays, with restocking art supplies and planning class events.

"I don't want you ever to move away," Lynn said softly.

"Don't worry. I don't intend to." Danielle's voice sounded brisk, but Lynn didn't miss the undertone of sadness.

Her friend was thinking about her husband, probably—the husband who had never been to Whitehorn, at least not as far as Lynn knew.

Danielle was now seeking a divorce. She was always vague about the details, would only say that it hadn't worked out. But Lynn sensed her friend still loved the man. From the few things Danielle had said about him, Lynn knew that once Danielle had been a very happily married woman. A woman deeply in love.

What would that be like? Lynn wondered as Danielle gently pushed her down onto the small cot in the corner and knelt at her feet, to slide off her brown flats and slip on the red shoes.

What would that be like?

To fall, as the saying went, truly, madly, *deeply* in love? Would it be worth the price, if a woman ended up like Danielle, starting over in another town, without the man she loved so much at her side?

Lynn reached out. Her hand touched Danielle's silky hair. Within the darkness of the blindfold, Lynn pictured Danielle's face, looking up at her, hazel eyes bright.

"A good friend. The best," Lynn whispered.

And Danielle whispered back, "You get what you give."

You get what you give. True words. But not absolute. Knowing Danielle, Lynn couldn't imagine she'd ever given her husband a moment's heartache. And yet, clearly, heartache had been his ultimate gift to her.

Maybe it was better to be like Lynn. Still a virgin on her twenty-fourth birthday. With no prospects of "truly, madly, deeply" anywhere in sight.

Then again, Danielle did have Sara. The adorable little chatterbox must go a long way toward making up for the heartache.

"Ready to see your new look?" Danielle asked. All traces of sadness had vanished from her voice. Now she sounded excited, anticipatory.

"I hope it's just half as good as you're acting like it is."

"Only one way to find out."

Lynn felt a sort of shimmer go through her body. A shimmer of anxiety—and of giddy expectancy. She held out her hand to be led back to the main room of the salon.

There was a full-length mirror on the wall opposite the door to the street. Danielle made Lynn wait, still blindfolded, while Gracie moved a potted fern out of the way.

Then, at last, Danielle untied the scarf, whipping it off with a magician's dramatic flourish. "Voilà!"

Everyone, including little Sara, began clapping and squealing.

"Do you love it?"

"Isn't it perfect?"

"You look incredible."

"Miss Taylor, you are *so* pretty!"

Lynn could only stare.

It was…magic. Real-life magic.

She didn't look like some glamorous, over-made-up stranger, as she had secretly feared that she might. She looked…exactly like herself.

Only better. A hundred times better. Everything was…enhanced. Made brighter. As if she had somehow been *fuzzy* before. A picture out of focus, now brought stunningly clear.

So very clear. Her skin glowed. Her hair shone. Her eyes were bigger, brighter, bluer than blue.

And the rest of her…

She couldn't believe it.

She turned, looked over her shoulder. The rear view was perfect, too. The red sweater dress clung lovingly to every newly slimmed-down curve, and the silver threads, woven so subtly through the cashmere, gleamed like tiny diamonds—or maybe a sprinkling of starlight—from the downy wool.

And the shoes. Why, the shoes didn't make her look too tall at all. She *was* tall. Why not make the most of it?

"Is that really me?" she heard herself whisper, turning and facing her reflection again.

"It's you!" crowed Sara. "Miss Taylor, it's really, really you! You're just like Cinderella, all ready for the ball."

Lynn couldn't help but agree. All those fairy-godmother jokes aside, she honestly did feel as if someone had cast a spell over her.

"This is…just magic." A wistful laugh escaped her. "Now all I need is for my prince to show up."

Lynn had barely finished speaking when the bell over the street door gave a jangle and Ross Garrison entered the salon.

Chapter Three

Ross Garrison was not a man who gaped.

But it took all the considerable self-control he possessed not to gawk like an idiot when he walked into the Whitehorn Salon and caught sight of Jennifer McCallum's teacher for the second time that day.

It couldn't be the same woman.

But it *was* the same woman.

Amazing.

Not that she hadn't possessed a certain wholesome, shyly dignified appeal before.

But now...

Now she was downright tempting.

Whoever had fixed her hair had worked wonders. Before, it had been a little longer, hadn't it? And a sort of brownish-blond color. Now it just brushed her shoulders and seemed shot with moonbeams. And those blue eyes. He'd thought them rather attractive before. He'd been struck by the way she had looked at him—with a careful reserve and with challenge, as well.

But now, enhanced as those eyes were with subtle shadows, they could take a man down to drowning.

He wanted to look away.

But he couldn't.

And Lynn couldn't look away, either.

Was this some dream she'd stumbled into? A heady, intoxicating dream, where suddenly a man like Ross Garrison stared at her—at *her*, plain, dependable Miss Taylor—as if she had captivated him?

Looking twice, that was what he was doing. Looking twice at *her*.

And maybe it was foolish of her. Foolish and shallow and silly.

But she *liked* the way he looked at her. She felt all fizzy and sparkling. Like a bottle of champagne with the cork just popped. And so…powerful, suddenly. In a purely female way.

Twenty-four years old today, she thought. And as of today, her entire experience with the opposite sex had consisted of awkward dates in college with boys as shy as she'd always been. But at that marvelous, special moment, Lynn Taylor was a siren. Her beauty could sink ships. Ross Garrison's stunned, frankly admiring stare told her so.

Speak up, damn it, Ross said to himself. All right. The kindergarten teacher has gotten to you. But you're no tongue-tied cowhand.

In his most self-assured tone, he broke the silence that had descended on the women at his entrance. "It's five o'clock, Ms. Taylor."

The little girl, Sara, grabbed her mother's hand and gave it a tug. "I thought you said he was a lawyer."

"Shh, honey, not now…"

"But we don't need a lawyer right now, Mommy. We need a *prince*."

All the women laughed at that—except the schoolteacher, whose glowing face turned a sweet, flustered pink. One of the two women Ross didn't know, probably the hairdresser, muttered under her breath, "I'd say he'll have to do," which caused another flurry of chuckles.

Danielle told her daughter, "I think you'd better go on back to your coloring books."

"But—"

"Go on now, Sara."

"Oh, all right." The little girl went over to a table in the corner and sat down.

Once the child was out of the way, all the women turned and looked at Ross again. He felt thoroughly outnumbered. And this wasn't a place where a man would feel all that comfortable, anyway. Maybe it was the excess of dried flower arrangements. There seemed to be one on the corner of every table, and they hung in wreaths and swags on the walls. Lace curtains draped the windows. The place smelled of women, too: perfume and powder, shampoo—and under everything, the harsh ammonialike scent of hair dyes and permanent waving solutions. He had no intention of interviewing Lynn Taylor there.

Dinner, he decided right then. He'd take her to dinner. At that new restaurant on State Street. Over a leisurely meal he could get past the hostility he'd sensed in her during their first meeting at the school.

He'd get her to open up to him, get her really talking about the child he'd been hired to represent.

Oh, come on, Garrison, taunted a cynical voice in the back of his mind. This is a fifteen-minute interview and a request for a short written report. You can do that over coffee at the Hip Hop Café across the street.

Ross tuned out that cynical voice. He gave the gorgeous blonde in the red dress his easiest, most casual smile. "Are you ready to go?"

Lynn hesitated. But not at the idea of leaving with him. Somehow, her reluctance to meet with him had faded away. She was thinking that she ought to change back into her regular clothes.

But no. She just couldn't bear to do that. Not right yet. Perhaps silver-threaded cashmere and two-inch red heels were unsuitable attire for a brief meeting with Jenny's new lawyer. But right then, Lynn didn't care.

She was keeping the dress on and the magic going. None of it was real, anyway. It was a dream she'd stepped into, a spell woven by the skilled hands of Gracie and Kim. She wanted to hold on to the magic. Just for a little while…

"You go on," Danielle was saying. "I'll bring you your other clothes tomorrow when I pick Sara up after school."

Gracie and Kim chorused their encouragement.

"Yes, you go ahead…."

"You go on, now…."

Danielle marched to the door and lifted Lynn's coat off the coatrack. "Here." She handed it to the lawyer, who obligingly held it open for Lynn to put on.

What else could she do?

She approached him, slid her arms into the sleeves and pulled it around herself, overly conscious of the light brush of his hands as he settled the garment onto her shoulders, thinking foolishly that even in heels she wasn't quite as tall as he was.

Danielle held out her purse. She took it. Ross Garrison opened the door again. He waited for Lynn to go through ahead of him.

And then she and the lawyer were standing on Center Street, side by side. A cold wind was blowing down from the Crazy Mountains north of town. Lynn shivered a little and wrapped her coat more closely around herself.

"Hungry?" he asked.

"Starved." And she was. She'd skipped lunch altogether. Forgotten all about it. But now that he had mentioned it, she was ready to eat. The Hip Hop was just across the street and two doors down. It was a charming little place, where everyone in town felt at home. She started toward it.

But Ross caught her elbow. "Come on. My Mercedes is just over there."

She didn't argue. His touch had distracted her, sending a sweet, zinging thrill along her nerves, making her shiver again—but this time not because of the wind.

He led her down the street about a hundred feet and then helped her into that Mercedes he'd mentioned, which was actually an SUV, of all things. She hadn't known that you could get a sports-utility version of a Mercedes, but there she was, sitting in the lovely leather seats, running her hand along the gleaming woodwork on her passenger-side door.

"It's not far, but we might as well drive," he said as the engine purred to life.

Ross took her to the State Street Grill, Whitehorn's newest and nicest restaurant, which had opened just last summer. There were hardly any other diners so early on a weekday evening, but he asked for a quiet corner table nonetheless.

And it was a lovely corner, shadowy and private. In the center of their table a single rose emerged, velvety-red, from a crystal vase. A pair of tall white candles flanked that rose. The waiter lighted them when he brought the wine list.

Ross studied the list and then glanced up at Lynn. "Any preferences?"

"I'm not much of a wine drinker, as a rule."

He was smiling—almost. "But you'll make an exception this once, won't you?"

Not wise, she chided herself silently. *A glass of wine is the last thing you need right now....*

But what she said was, "Well, to tell you the truth, it *is* my birthday."

That almost-smile deepened. "Seriously?"

She nodded.

And he said, "Then we'll have champagne." The waiter hovered at his elbow. Ross turned to him and said the name of something French.

A few minutes later, he was lifting a flute glass full of the golden, bubbly stuff. "To you, Ms. Lynn Taylor. Happy birthday." She held up her own glass until it met his with a bright-sounding clink.

The fizzy wine shimmered down her throat and made a warm glow in her stomach. They took a min-

ute to order—appetizers, salads and the main course.
Then the waiter disappeared.

Ross leaned toward her across the table. "So tell
me…"

She set her glass on the snowy cloth, made a low,
questioning sound.

"This new look of yours…"

She was not a woman prone to teasing, but right
then, teasing seemed to come to her as naturally as
breathing. She raised one newly reshaped eyebrow.
"New look?"

He chuckled. "What? You didn't think I'd noticed?"

She confessed with a small laugh, "I noticed. That
you noticed…"

"Good. We're clear on that much."

"Yes, I suppose we are."

"Then what brought on this change?"

She sipped again, felt that lovely fizziness slide
down her throat. "It's my birthday present from
Danielle. And Gracie and Kim, too."

"Gracie and Kim. They would be the other two
women, in the salon?"

"Yes. The owner and her daughter."

"And what did the little girl mean, with that remark about the prince?"

Funny, she'd felt her cheeks flame back in the
shop when Sara had announced so bluntly, "We
need a prince." But she didn't feel the least embarrassed now.

She told him. Simply and directly. About how
Danielle had called her early that morning with birthday greetings and instructions to be ready after class,
to bring her new red dress and red high-heeled shoes.

"She wouldn't tell me then what the surprise was going to be. She only said, 'Just call me your fairy godmother.'"

"As in Cinderella?"

"That's right. It got to be kind of a joke. Me as Cinderella. And Danielle and Gracie and Kim as my fairy godmothers, waving a magic wand over me. Then, once they'd worked their magic, I said that all I needed was a prince."

"Then I showed up." The candlelight gleamed, two spots of soft gold, in his dark eyes.

"Um-hmm. Right on time."

"But not a prince." He put on a look of great regret. "Only a lawyer…"

Lynn picked up her flute again. "Sometimes a girl has to make do with whomever shows up."

"Whomever," he repeated. "You just proved you're still a schoolteacher, after all."

She sipped. "Yes. And I'm warning you…"

"Don't tell me. At midnight, you turn into a pumpkin."

"Much worse. At midnight, I give you a pop quiz."

"I see."

"Then I make you recite your *ABC*s."

"And then?"

She considered. "Times tables. Yes. Right up through ten times ten. And from there, I'll want to see how you do at conjugating verbs."

"It sounds terrifying."

"It would be. But luckily for you, we'll have said good-night long before then."

"Yes. Luckily for me…"

They shared a long look. A much too intimate look.

Lynn reminded herself that they were only here to talk about Jenny.

But then, before she could say anything to get them going on the topic of her student, their appetizers appeared.

He asked her where she went to college.

"Montana State," she replied. "Major in education, minor in English. How about you?"

He said he'd gone to Princeton on a scholarship. "I was miserable there. Didn't know anybody. They'd all come from Ivy League prep schools. To them, I was just a cowboy, manure still on my boots, fresh out of high school in Billings."

"But you stuck it out."

"Damn right. Then I went on to law school in Colorado."

"And got your law degree when you were— what?"

"I took the bar exam when I was twenty-four."

"That's pretty young, isn't it?"

"I knew what I wanted. To make it and make it big. I hired on with Turow, Travis and Lindstrom, a major Denver law firm, right away."

Trish, who spent her lunch hours at the Hip Hop collecting every tidbit she could on Ross Garrison, had mentioned that he'd come from Denver. "And then?"

His eyes turned cold. "I worked my way up the food chain."

"At Turow, Travis and—?"

"Lindstrom. Right. I advanced there with alarming rapidity. I was twenty-eight when I made partner. It was an unheard-of accomplishment.'' The irony in his tone matched the chill in his eyes, making it seem that the ''accomplishment'' he spoke of was actually nothing of the kind.

Lynn had the strangest urge—to reach across the table. To lay her hand over his. To say something gentle and understanding, something that would bring warmth to his eyes.

She kept her hands to herself. And he finished, ''I stayed with the firm until a little over a year ago, when I decided it was time for a change.''

Time for a change, she thought, and knew there was more to it than that. Trish had mentioned a divorce. A broken heart Trish intended to mend...

Lynn studied him across the table, admitting to herself that, beyond this foolish and dangerous game of flirtation she was playing with him, she had started to like him, to respond to him on some deeper level—which she knew she shouldn't allow herself to do.

He was too rich. And too sophisticated. And even though he seemed to have zero romantic interest in Trish, her sister had set her sights on him. Trish would never consider Lynn any kind of competition. But still, there would be nothing but trouble in the family if Trish thought Lynn had dared to make a play for him.

And yet, here she was in this fancy restaurant, drinking champagne with him. And flirting. Showing off her smart mouth, as Jewel always used to say whenever her usually self-effacing stepdaughter had the bad judgment to let that particular side of herself shine through.

They should talk about Jenny.

And they would, of course. Very soon. But really, there was no great hurry. She raised her glass to her lips and sipped more champagne.

A few minutes later, the main course arrived. Filet mignon. Fork-tender. It literally melted in her mouth.

She'd just swallowed the first scrumptious bite when Ross warned in a whisper, "Don't look now, but I think—yes. She's spotted us."

"Who?"

"Lily Mae Wheeler. She's headed our way. I'll give you a little free legal advice."

"What?"

"Don't tell her anything, unless you want the whole town to know."

Lynn had no time to reply. Lily Mae was upon them. "My Lord, Lynn Taylor! Honey, I hardly did recognize you." Lynn smiled gamely up at Whitehorn's most notorious gossip. "You look sweet as a heifer in a field of new clover. I *love* your hair." Copper bracelets jangling, Lily Mae patted her own teased and heavily sprayed coiffure, which was auburn at the moment. "Maybe *I* should try blond again. What do you think?"

"I do like the auburn," Lynn said judiciously.

Lily Mae left off patting her hair and patted Lynn's shoulder instead. "Sweet, sweet girl. You always say just the right thing." False eyelashes batted Ross's way. "And *hello,* Mr. Garrison. How are you this brisk October evening?"

"I'm just fine, Mrs. Wheeler."

"Enjoying that beautiful new house of yours?"

"I am. Very much."

"It's up along Route 17, isn't it? On Black Bear Lake."

"Yes."

"I confess, Winona Cobbs has told me all about it. She has to drive by there to get into town." Winona Cobbs lived in a trailer out at the end of Route 17. She ran her own peculiar enterprise there known as the Stop 'n Swap. She kept bees and was considered by many to possess psychic powers. She was also almost as big a gossip as Lily Mae.

Lily Mae forged on. "And I heard you've been hired by the Kincaid estate."

"That's right," Ross said.

Lily Mae clucked her tongue. "Wasn't that just a terrible shame—about Wendell? There are many who don't believe it now, but once, Wendell Hargrove was an honorable man. It was after his dear wife, Alice, died that the trouble started. He just couldn't cope with the loss. He developed that gambling problem. And then he—well, I suppose you know all of this."

"I've heard the facts, yes."

"And now you're representing our Jenny."

"That's right."

"You do a good job for her, now."

"I will, Mrs. Wheeler. I promise you."

Lily Mae turned on Lynn again. "Hon, I mean it. Your face. Your hair. That gorgeous dress. I do truly love to see a woman make the most of what she's got. And when that woman is *you,* well, all I can say is, it is about time."

Lynn murmured a thank-you; it seemed the safest way to go.

Lily Mae spotted the ice bucket and the bottle nestled in it. "And what's this? Champagne?" Her painted-on brows went so high, they threatened to vanish beneath the hard fringe of hair on her forehead. "A special occasion?" She waved a carmine-tipped hand, causing more clattering. "Never mind. Of course it is. It's always a special occasion when an eligible man and a beautiful single woman enjoy a fine meal together...although I must admit, I had thought—" Lily Mae actually cut herself off. "But never mind about that."

"About what?" Lynn asked, regretting the question immediately.

But Lily Mae surprised her. "Oh, nothing."

It wasn't *nothing,* and Lynn knew it. She could see the truth in Lily Mae's over-made-up eyes. The sweet-hearted gossip knew that Trish was after Ross. How could she not know? Who other than Lily Mae would Trish have been pumping for information about the new lawyer in town?

"Really, hon. It was nothing at all," Lily Mae repeated. "Sometimes I do run on, and that is a plain fact." Then she chuckled. "And now I am going to leave you. I've a dear friend in town from Billings for the night. She's in the Ladies right now. I'll tell you what, I won't even interrupt you again to introduce her, because I can see that the two of you want to be alone."

Lynn opened her mouth to protest that remark, but Ross caught her eye before she spoke. She read his look: What's the point?

She had to agree with him. Lily Mae Wheeler would think what she wanted to think. And anything Lynn said to her would only give her an excuse to stay and chat longer.

"Enjoy those filets," said Lily Mae. "Don't they just turn right to butter inside your mouth?"

"Yes," Lynn agreed. "They're delicious."

With a last jingling wave, Lily Mae trotted off.

Ross watched her go. After a moment, he said, "You'll be relieved to know the hostess is leading her to a table in the far corner, behind a pillar. She won't be flashing all those capped teeth and shaking her bracelets at us through the rest of the meal, after all."

Lynn felt she had to speak up on Lily Mae's behalf. "She has a good heart."

Ross shook his head. "But we'll be an 'item' by tomorrow. When she gets to her regular table at the Hip Hop and starts spreading the news."

And what will Trish say when she hears?

Lynn decided not to think about that. It would work out. She'd explain to her sister that they'd needed to talk about Jenny. Which was the truth.

Ross picked up his fork again. "It doesn't matter, does it, what Lily Mae Wheeler thinks or says? *We* know the real situation, after all. And it's not as if we've been caught doing anything but enjoying a meal together."

Their eyes met. She sighed. "You're right. There'll be a little talk. And then, when we don't see each other again, the talk will die down."

"Right." He said the word very low. And then, for several nerve-racking seconds, he said nothing more, only looked at her, making her pulse pound too fast and her face feel overly warm.

At last he shrugged. "Being talked about is the price you pay for living in a town like Whitehorn, where everyone knows everyone else's business."

"Exactly." Carefully she cut a bite of meat and slipped the delicious morsel between her lips.

Ross watched her. He liked watching her. Liked it way too much.

Yes. Too much. Those were the operative words here. He liked watching her too much, was enjoying himself too much.

He should call a halt right now.

This was not going to go anywhere. Lynn Taylor might seem a temptress tonight, but he knew damn well that she was an innocent at heart.

She didn't want what he wanted, which was to sit here for another hour or so and look at her some more. To listen to her slightly throaty voice, to catch an occasional whiff of that enticing perfume she wore.

Then, when they'd lingered over the meal for much longer than they should have, he wanted to take her home. To his bed. Where he would enjoy her all the more.

Until the night was over. At which time, he would want her to go back to her own life and leave him to his.

And she would want…what? He couldn't say for sure. But hadn't she just as much as told him she was looking for a prince?

Ross Garrison was no prince. And nothing was going to happen between him and Lynn Taylor.

Looked at from just about any angle, seducing her would be a fool's move.

He'd seen the way Danielle Mitchell treated her. And those two hairdressers, too. Even Lily Mae Wheeler. Everyone in Whitehorn loved Lynn Taylor. They all seemed to feel protective toward her.

He had a practice to build here. And seducing the

town innocent was not going to help him create trust with potential clients.

He should eat his steak, ask his few questions about his young client, pay the check and take the woman back to her car.

Unfortunately, though, for some insane reason, he couldn't bear to let her go. Not quite yet.

She glanced up from her meal and asked softly, "You *do* like it here in Whitehorn, don't you?"

"Yes. I do."

"You said you were raised in Billings?"

"Right."

"Why didn't you move back there, when you were…ready for a change?"

"I have no family there anymore. My folks have been dead for several years now."

"No brothers or sisters?"

"One of each. But we're not close. And they've moved away, too. My sister lives in Salt Lake City. And my brother's in Southern California now. Works for some electronics firm, I think."

She picked up her water glass. Her champagne flute was empty. He checked the bottle—empty, too. "I'll order another one."

"No." She drank, set the water glass down. "Better not." He upended the bottle in its bucket of ice as she started to slide her napkin in at the side of her plate.

He could see the end of the evening in those eyes of hers.

"Dessert," he said. "You have to have dessert."

"Oh." Her eyelashes fluttered down, then lifted again. "No more. Really." A busman appeared and whisked their plates away.

Ross waited for him to leave before coaxing, "It *is* your birthday, after all. And they have something really special here. Dark chocolate truffle cake. It's my own personal weakness, I have to admit."

"Truffle cake." She considered. And she did it charmingly, tipping her head to the side, touching the tip of her tongue to the corner of her lip for an instant, as if she could actually taste a bit of chocolate there.

What would it feel like, to touch his own tongue to those lips of hers? Good, he imagined. Very, very good…

She drew in a breath. "No. I'm not hungry anymore. Not hungry at all."

He should have just let it go at that. But he didn't. "So what? It's chocolate. Eat it for…the pleasure of it. And because it's your birthday."

She stared at him. Awareness, and of much more than the temptation of chocolate, seemed to weave itself around them like a net of silk—or like the silver threads in that dress of hers, subtle, but so damn seductive.

Then she blinked. "No." Her voice was firmer now. "I really don't want dessert."

Time to call for the check. But he didn't. "Well, you'll wait for me, won't you, if I want some?"

"Of course."

"Coffee?"

"I'd love some."

He signaled the waiter and whispered in the man's ear.

"What did you tell him?" she demanded when the waiter had hurried off.

"Guess."

She laughed again. God, he really did like the sound of her laugh.

"I know what you did. You told him it was my birthday, didn't you?"

"Guilty as charged."

"Oh, Ross..."

It was the first time she'd called him Ross. He liked the way his name sounded on her lips. Liked it far too much.

"You can blow out the candle," he said. "And I'll eat the cake."

Three waiters appeared, singing the birthday song.

They marched to the table, and put the slice of cake with its single candle in front of her. The song ended. Delicately she blew out the flame.

"Happy birthday!" the waiters chorused one more time.

"Oh, thank you," she said, giggling like a kid and clapping her hands.

The waiters served the coffee, then made themselves scarce.

Lynn plucked the candle from the cake, set it on a side dish and slid the plate across to him. "There you go. Indulge yourself."

He picked up his fork. "You *sure* you won't have any?"

"Don't you start in again."

"Just one little bite...?" He pressed the side of the fork down through the layers of chocolate shavings, snow-white icing, dark cake, and that impossible, silky whipped-truffle center. "I'm telling you, this tastes as good as it looks." He held up the fork.

She wrinkled her nose at him. "Do you ever quit?"

"Never. It's not in my nature."

She looked at the fork and the bite of cake balanced there. "If I taste it, will you leave me alone?"

"Unless you beg me for more."

"I won't."

It sounded to him like a challenge. An utterly erotic one.

A challenge he had to keep telling himself he would not accept.

"Yes or no?" he dared in return.

And she did it.

She leaned forward. He gave her the cake, watching those soft lips open to take it in.

Her eyes closed. "Umm." Her mouth moved as she tasted it, savored the heady mix of rich flavors. She swallowed.

"More?"

"No, thank you."

He held her eyes for a moment, that silken web of awareness spinning, dizzily now, all around them. And then he lowered the fork and took a bite for himself.

Enjoy it, Garrison, he told himself. Imagine you can taste her, in the cream and the chocolate, on the silver prongs of this fork. It's all you're going to have of her. Because she's not going to beg for more. And you're not going to push her.

You want only a single night.

And she...

She's looking for a prince.

Too soon, the cake was nothing but a few crumbs on a china plate. He signaled for the check and signed for it. The waiter brought her coat, started to hold it up for her.

Jealous of every last touch, Ross rose from his chair. "Here." The waiter handed it over.

Lynn stood and he helped her into it, as he had once before, in that shop with all the women watching, taking longer this time than he needed to, because the scent of her, the reality of her, was right there—too close, and much too tempting. His knuckles brushed cashmere and burned.

Silently he called himself a number of crude names.

He was hard. Had been since the moment she took his fork into her mouth. Fully aroused, like some green kid who couldn't keep it down even in public. At least his jacket covered the bulge.

Once she had the coat on, he put his hand at the small of her back, under the pretense of guiding her toward the door. But she didn't really need guiding. She knew damn well where the door was. He put his hand on her so that he could feel her, the softness, the womanflesh of her, under all the layers of clothing that protected her from him.

The hostess murmured, "Have a nice evening, Mr. Garrison," as they passed the reservation podium.

He nodded. "Good night."

They were out the door, standing on the street in the darkness with the icy Montana wind blowing down from the mountains, before he remembered that he'd yet to bring up the matter of Jennifer McCallum.

Chapter Four

She turned to him, clutching her coat against the chilling fingers of the wind. "I wonder if you could drive me back to the school. I left my Blazer there."

"Wait a minute." He sounded every bit as offhand as he'd intended to. Not at all the way he felt, which was way too aroused. Too hungry—and not for filet mignon or truffle cake. For her.

He wanted to reach for her, right there. To yank her body against his, shove his hands into her moon-silvered hair—and finally taste that mouth that had teased him so thoroughly with throaty laughter and clever words. That mouth, which had taken cake straight from his own fork.

"Brr…" She hunched her shoulders down into her collar. "Wait for what?"

"We still haven't talked about my client."

She started to speak, then saw the two cowboys

ambling toward them on the street. The men were dressed in regulation Whitehorn: worn jeans, battered boots, sweat-stained hats and shearling jackets. Lynn smiled at them, murmured two names in greeting.

The men stopped in their tracks. They stared at Lynn, mouths slightly agape. Ross would have laughed—if he hadn't wanted to kill both of them with his bare hands. He knew what they were thinking. He'd thought it himself. She looked good. Too damn good. Like something a man could start in with and never get enough of.

One of the cowboys gulped. "Uh, *Miss Taylor?*"

She laughed that throaty, maddening laugh. "Yes, Eddie, it's me."

"Well. Uh. Hi, there."

They both tipped their hats.

"Hello yourself," she said. She asked the other one, whose name was Tom, how his sister was doing.

"Lindy's feelin' better now, Miss Taylor."

"Well, I'm pleased to hear that. You tell her to take it easy. Pneumonia's nothing to fool with."

"I will, Miss Taylor. I surely will. And you have yourself a nice day…I mean, night."

"Thank you, Tom. Same to you."

They both tipped their hats again, this time in Ross's general direction. He gave them a curt nod. And then—finally—they went on by.

She turned to him. "It always makes me smile. This is only my second year as a teacher at Whitehorn Elementary, but still, everyone in town, even the people I went to high school with, call me Miss Taylor."

It didn't seem all that damn funny to him. Those

cowboys had better call her Miss Taylor, as far as Ross was concerned.

She was still smiling. "Tom and Eddie work the Birchley place. That's north of town, between the No Bull Ranch and the—"

"I know where the Birchley spread is." He didn't, not really. And he also didn't need to hear another word about Tom and Eddie, who should learn not to stare at a woman as if they damn well had never seen one before.

She moved a step away from him. "Is something wrong?"

"No." He fisted his hands at his sides—to keep them from reaching out and pulling her back. "Not a thing." He dragged in a slow breath and ordered the bulge in his pants to subside.

"Are you *sure* you're all right?"

"I'm fine. And we really do still have to talk."

"Well, I know, but—"

"We could stop by my house...." Once the suggestion was out, he could hardly believe he'd made it.

And apparently, neither could she. "Your house?" Her enchanting face showed both dismay—and excitement.

"It's not that far. You can have one last cup of coffee. Then I'll take you home."

"I…" She hesitated. He knew with heart-stopping certainty that she would tell him no. But then relief hollowed him out as she finished, "I'll still need to get my Blazer."

"Fine, then. I'll take you back to the school as soon as we're finished." He glanced at his watch. Still early. Good. "It's only a little after seven.

You'll be home by eight-thirty—nine at the latest."
One more hour. Or two. No harm in that.

Yes, all right. It was playing with fire. But damn
it, he hadn't felt like this in...

Come to think of it, maybe he'd never felt exactly
like this in his life. And he'd been alone for too long
now. Had he been lonely? All right, maybe he had.
He'd thought he wanted it that way. But tonight, just
for a little while, he only wanted this magic to con-
tinue.

Magic. Yes, that was the word. All the talk of fairy
godmothers and spells had gotten to him. *She* had
gotten to him, with those innocent blue eyes and that
red dress, her tart tongue and that maddening perfume.

He knew himself. Knew that whatever this feeling
was, it wouldn't last. But for right now, for an hour
or so, he just didn't want to let her go.

Lynn's thoughts were moving along similar lines.
She knew as well as Ross did that going to his house
was taking this risky flirtation one step too far. But
still...

It was her birthday. Her special, magical Cinderella birthday. Tonight, for the first time in her life,
she was living a fairy tale. She was Cinderella at the
ball, Sleeping Beauty awakened and ugly-duckling-
turned-swan all rolled into one.

Don't let it end yet, she kept thinking. Not yet.
Oh, not quite yet...

He put his hand at her back, as he'd done in the
restaurant. She felt that touch through every fiber of
her being. "Come on," he said. "It's too cold to
stand here on the street a minute longer. Let's go."

* * *

The house was five miles northeast of town, perched on a rocky ledge that led down to Black Bear Lake. A soaring structure of rough-hewn spruce logs and tall, gleaming windows, it was surrounded by stately fir trees.

Ross led her inside, took her coat and purse and put them in the closet near the front door. Then he ushered her into a massive great room, where the floor-to-ceiling fireplace was made of big smooth stones—collected from the eastern slopes of the Rockies, he told her. There was a mantel of sorts, a heavy wooden shelf, built into the stones. And a big clock on the mantel. A clock that said it was 7:36.

Ross took a minute to open the fireplace insert and strike a match to the logs already laid over kindling within.

As she waited for him to light the fire, Lynn admired the room. Overhead, huge logs formed the spokes of a giant arching wheel. The furniture around her looked inviting. It was upholstered in deep brown leather and jewel-toned chenille. Out the big windows, through the lacy branches of the firs, she could see the darkly gleaming waters of the lake.

He offered coffee. "Or maybe you'd prefer brandy?"

She decided on the brandy. The very idea of it was just so lovely and decadent. She'd never been a woman who drank brandy. Until tonight.

At the far end of the room, and at a right angle to the fireplace, there was a long bar that divided the kitchen from the dining area. Ross went around behind the bar and took a bottle from a cabinet. From the rack overhead he removed two big balloon-shaped glasses, the kind made just for sipping brandy.

Once he'd poured them each a glass, he gave her a tour. He led her first to his downstairs study with its own library of gold-tooled leather books, then through two bedrooms off the great room, each with its own private bath—and finally up the wide rough-hewn stairs and down a hall.

They glanced into two more bedrooms. Then came the master suite, which was almost as big as the great room downstairs and faced northwest.

Lynn followed him into the room, where rich-colored kilim rugs covered the hardwood floors. His bed was king-size, of heavy, dark wood. In the sitting area the leather chairs were deeply tufted, finished with nailhead trim. Western art and a few rare-looking Indian tapestries adorned the rough-textured walls. Right then, the huge windows showed only the stars and the shadowy forms of the Crazy Mountains in the distance. But in daylight, the view of blue sky and snow-capped mountains would be breathtaking.

She murmured, "Oh, Ross. It's just beautiful."

He gave her his rueful smile and ran a forefinger along the surface of a mahogany table. "Dusty, though. My housekeeper is as useless as my secretary." He didn't realize his mistake until the words were already out.

Just like that, the lovely mood fizzled and faded.

Ross's smile faded, too. He shook his head. "That was a stupid thing to say."

Lynn felt as if a large hand had reached out and shaken her, jarring her cruelly from a sweet and impossible dream. What in the world was she doing here, in a rich man's bedroom after dark, a glass of brandy in her hand?

She heard herself asking, "Is Trish…really all that bad?"

He didn't immediately reply, but from the grim set of his mouth she could guess what he was thinking. Finally he allowed, "She's only—what? Twenty-two? That's pretty young."

She knew she should let it go at that. But somehow, she couldn't. "You didn't answer my question."

His expression turned pained. "Look, I—" He paused, then admitted, "I'm sorry. I know you're loyal to your sister. But the simple fact is, she's not working out."

It was much worse than that, though Ross didn't say so.

The real truth was, Trish Taylor was driving him right up the wall.

He probably should have known the girl was hopeless from the first. But then, he was accustomed to working in a major firm, where Personnel carefully screened applicants before he ever talked to them.

At first meeting, she'd seemed bright; she'd lacked experience, but he'd thought she would learn fast. And she was attractive. When he'd interviewed her, she'd worn a nice dark blue business suit; her looks, he'd decided, would be a real plus in terms of an office image. How could he have known that as soon as Trish Taylor had the job, she'd go back to the too-short denim skirts and the dangling Lily Mae Wheeler-type earrings she obviously preferred?

And her office skills?

She didn't have any. The girl had graduated from

business school in Bozeman. Her résumé had claimed she knew shorthand and typed sixty words a minute. Unfortunately, she couldn't seem to decipher her shorthand after she took it. And he'd seen her type. *He* could type faster, using only two fingers. She was always losing files—in her desktop computer and in the row of legal-sized file cabinets that lined the wall to the right of her work area.

Lynn was looking down into the amber depths of her brandy. "Maybe if you talked to her…?"

God, he did not want to discuss this with her.

But she wouldn't give it up—any more than she would look into his eyes right then. "Ross. Have you talked to her?"

"Yes. I have."

He'd talked to Trish, all right. More than once. A week ago he'd finally told her frankly that she'd better concentrate harder on her work—or look for another job. It hadn't done any good.

Ross knew the main problem; he'd have to be blind, deaf and dumb *not* to know it. Trish Taylor had a flaming crush on him. Instead of doing her job, she spent her working hours gazing off into nowhere with dreamy eyes, blushing every time he asked her to bring him a file and scheming over new ways to get him chatting about his private life.

Secretary falls for boss. The oldest cliché in the book. Except the way the cliché usually went, the secretary actually knew how to type. And she also had the tact and grace never to let her feelings show unless she received some indication that they might be returned. Not so with Trish Taylor.

And Lynn still wasn't looking at him.

"Are you going to stare into that glass forever?"

he asked, trying for a light tone and not succeeding all that well.

Lynn made herself look into his eyes again.

This is totally inappropriate, she told herself. Inappropriate and unacceptable. I should not be standing here in this man's bedroom, sipping his brandy, while he tells me he's going to fire my sister any day now.

"I think we'd better go back downstairs." She spun on her heel and headed for the hall.

"Lynn."

She froze, but she didn't turn around.

He spoke to her back. "There is nothing at all between your sister and me. I'm her boss and she's my employee. And that's all."

"It's none of my business." She tried to start walking again.

And again he said, "Lynn."

"What?" She whirled back to face him then, glaring.

"Do you believe me?"

"What does it matter?"

"It matters."

She lifted her chin, drew herself up to her full five foot eleven in heels. "Why?"

"I might not be the prince you're looking for, but I would never have brought you here if there was something going on between your sister and me."

She kept glaring at him. She wanted so badly to be angry with him. But she wasn't, not really. At least, not any angrier than she was with herself. She drew a calming breath and let it out slowly. "You *shouldn't* have brought me here. And I shouldn't have come."

What else could he say but "I know."

"Then *why* did you bring me here?" She threw out the question as a desperate challenge.

He didn't answer, only looked at her with eyes that promised things she shouldn't let herself understand—shocking things, intimate things. Things she'd never done before. Things she probably never *would* do. Things that, if she ever *did* do, she wouldn't do with him.

Would she?

"Why?" she demanded again, to distract herself from the dangerous turn her own thoughts had taken. "Why did you bring me here?" She was hoping against hope that he would lie, say something tactful and easy, something to make everything right again, make everything safe.

Instead, he told the truth on a low husk of breath. "I brought you here because I couldn't bear to let you go."

She stared at him. She felt hot all over, suddenly. Her heart pounded hard and hurtfully, so loud to her own ears she was sure he must hear it.

Get out, her wiser self insisted. Get out of here. Now.

She backed away another step, enough to clear the doorway, so she was standing in the hall next to a narrow mahogany table with curving claw-footed legs.

"Lynn."

She froze again.

And he asked the question she didn't want to hear. "Why did you agree to come here with me?"

"I..."

"I answered you. Now answer me. Why?"

Her mouth worked, but no words came out. She watched him, unable, somehow, to break the hold of his eyes and get out of there. He started walking toward her, eating up the space between them with slow, deliberate strides.

Go, move, turn, run! her good sense shouted in her ear. But something else—a vivid longing that pulsed through her in heated, needful waves—held her there until he reached her.

He took her glass, set it on the claw-footed table. He set his own glass down there, too. Then he cupped her chin in both of his big, fine hands.

"Why did you come here?" he demanded, so softly this time. The feel of his hands on her skin was pure heaven. His breath touched her upturned face, melted something inside her.

"I..."

"Yes?" Urgent. He sounded urgent. Her own body seemed to answer that urgency with an erotic insistence all its own.

"Tell me." He brushed his lips across hers. Oh, that felt lovely. She wished he'd do it again.

Maybe he would if she confessed the truth. "I didn't want the night to end." Her voice was a throaty whisper. "It was wrong of me. So foolish..."

"But you came here anyway."

"Yes. Because it's my birthday. And it's all been like magic. And I didn't want it to be over, I didn't want midnight to strike."

"But it will." His eyes looked sad now, sad and knowing. "Midnight does that," he whispered. "It always comes. Eventually." He ran his hands down her throat, an encompassing caress that made her heart stutter in her chest.

Then he took her shoulders, gently and resolutely. "Do you want me to take you home now?"

"No." The word got out before she could stop it. And then once it *was* out, she accepted the fact that it was only the truth.

A smile played on his lips for a moment and was gone. "Then what *do* you want?"

"I want…" She gulped, then made herself tell him. "First, I want to know for certain. Is there any hope, any hope at all that you and Trish might—"

He shook his head before she could finish. "I meant what I said. Your sister is my secretary. That's all."

She believed him. She'd known it all along, really. But it seemed terribly important that she make absolutely sure.

"What else?" he prompted, running his hands down her arms and back up again, a slow, warm caress that wreaked havoc on her thought processes.

She managed to whisper, "If we…" and then felt her face flushing hot and red. Oh, she could not go on.

"If we what?"

"If I…" She gulped again. She'd never been a liar, but right now she was thinking of the lies she might tell, thinking that yes, Lily Mae Wheeler had seen them drinking champagne at the State Street Grill, but that no one knew she had actually come to his house with him. That it was still early yet.

True, Trish lived with her in the family home that Lynn's father had left to Lynn in his will. Since Lynn always came home early, Trish would definitely notice if she suddenly returned very late.

But if she didn't stay *too* late…

And if she got Danielle to cover for her, to say…

Oh, sweet Lord, what was she doing?

It was wrong, terribly wrong, what she was letting herself imagine. And she would have to face hell, from her sister *and* her community—or tell an ugly string of lies—to get away with it.

And where would it go, anyway, if she *did* get away with it?

She had seen the coldness in his eyes when he talked of that law firm in Denver. She knew about his divorce, that it had not been a friendly one.

There was something…hard about him. Something closed in. She'd broken through that hardness tonight, with the help of a red dress and the strange, heady power her new look had given her.

But a woman would have a big job for herself, getting through his defenses on any long-lasting basis. What made her dare to imagine that she would be the one to accomplish such a feat?

Underneath the temporary glamour, she was still the same woman she'd always been: plain, reserved Lynn Taylor. The kindergarten teacher, born to be addressed as "Miss." A woman at whom men like this one never looked twice.

Tomorrow she'd put on her regular clothes and her flat shoes. With the help of the diagram and the makeup samples Kim had given her, she might try to recreate some semblance of the magic. But it wouldn't be the same.

And his defenses would go back up.

No, spending the night with him—making *love* with him, because that's what they'd be doing—was impossible. She was a teacher, for heaven's sake. There were certain moral standards that the people of Whitehorn rightfully expected her to uphold. When and if she ever did make love with a man, she planned to be married to him first. She couldn't just fall into bed with someone she'd met face-to-face only that afternoon.

Lynn could hardly believe she kept letting herself consider it, kept thinking how much she *wanted* it, wanted him to kiss her—a real, deep, all-consuming kiss. Wanted his fine hands caressing her, all over her body. Wanted—

She heard a chiming sound, faint but still discernible, coming from downstairs. The clock on the mantel. Announcing the hour.

It was eight o'clock.

Chapter Five

Just as Lynn was about to step back from him, Ross dropped his hands away and stepped back himself.

Something deep inside her cried out in hungry bewilderment at the loss of his touch, at the sudden absence of his body, which had been so deliciously, temptingly close.

She resolutely ignored that silent cry.

He said, "I'm sorry. This is foolish, just as you said."

"Yes." She made her head bob up and down to show how much she agreed with him. "We'd better go downstairs."

"And talk a little about my client," he continued for her.

"And then you can take me to the school."

He picked up her brandy and handed it to her. Then he took his own. "Come on. Let's go."

* * *

Ross shrugged out of his jacket when they got downstairs. He tossed it over a chair and they sat in front of the fire, on either end of one of those comfortable chenille sofas.

"Now," she said in a businesslike tone. "What do you want to know about Jenny?"

"I want background, that's all. Just tell me about her. What you know of her history, what you've observed from contact with her."

"Truthfully, Ross, I'm sure I don't have anything to say that you haven't already heard."

"Let me be the judge of that."

So she shared what she knew.

Jennifer McCallum, natural daughter of Jeremiah Kincaid and Mary March, adopted child of Jessica and Sterling McCallum, had been through a lot in her five years of life. At first she was a mystery baby, found abandoned on the steps of the Kincaid ranch house. And then an evil woman intent on stealing her birthright had kidnapped her. Fortunately, Jenny had been rescued unharmed and the kidnapper had been caught. Then, at the age of three, Jenny was stricken with leukemia. For a time, they'd all believed she would die. But her long-lost half brother, Wayne Kincaid, had stepped forward, a perfect match for the bone marrow transplant that had saved Jenny's life.

"Now," Lynn told Ross, "her health is stabilized—which I'm sure her doctor has told you."

"Yes," he said. "That's what I understood."

"She's doing very well in school, which I think I already mentioned."

"You did, that's true." He laughed. He

seemed…totally relaxed now. And she felt relaxed, too. Those dangerous moments upstairs seemed long ago and far away, as if they had happened between two other people.

"What else?" he prompted.

She thought for a moment. "Well, socially, she's a dream. Friendly and outgoing. You wouldn't believe to talk to her that she's ever been treated with anything but gentleness and love."

"You're saying she makes friends easily?"

"That's an understatement. You must have heard what they call her. The darling of Whitehorn. It may sound corny, but it's the truth. She is just that."

"And she and Sara Mitchell…?"

"As Sara told you, the two are best friends." Lynn chuckled. "They spend every moment they can together. And they won't stop trading their personal belongings. Snack boxes and art supply cases, sweaters and hair clips. You name it. At first I tried to keep the trading under control. But since neither Danielle nor the McCallums seem bothered by it, I've gotten so I just let it go. It pleases them so. And in the end, everything equals out. Or at least, that's what I tell myself…."

His gaze scanned her face. "The two of them, Sara and Jennifer, they're your favorites, aren't they?"

Was her preference that obvious? She tried to look stern. "A good teacher doesn't play favorites."

"Still, deep in your heart, you feel something special for them."

After what had transpired upstairs, she wasn't sure if she should be telling this particular man about anything that came from "deep in her heart."

But then again, they'd pulled themselves back

from the brink, hadn't they? They had a tacit understanding now. She would give him the information he sought—and then he would drive her to her car.

It was only Jenny and Sara they were discussing now. Nothing risky. Nothing really personal.

She wanted to shuck off her pretty shoes, to get a little more comfortable. And why not? She'd just slide them back on when it was time to go.

She pushed the shoes off, tucked her legs up to the side and teasingly warned, "You have to promise never to tell a soul."

He set down his brandy glass on the coffee table and raised his right hand, palm out. "You have my solemn word. Now confess. *Are* they your favorites?"

She let out a big, playful sigh. "Yes, I'm afraid that they are."

"Why?"

"Why not? They're both adorable. They love school. They're so…happy with the world. So *interested* in everything. So curious. And so verbal." She made a show of rolling her eyes. "Boy. Is Sara ever verbal."

"But there's more to it than that."

She lifted one shoulder in a hint of a shrug. "No, I don't think so. And anyway, isn't that enough?"

"Come on. They're blond and blue-eyed, bright and talkative. Just like you."

"Like me?" She frowned. "No, they—"

He cut in before she could finish. "They remind you of yourself at that age, don't they?"

A scoffing sound escaped her. "Of *myself?* Haven't you looked at them? They're beautiful little girls."

"You're beautiful, too." He said the words bluntly. Flatly. A statement of fact.

"Well, tonight…I mean, I guess I'm different tonight. Not my real self."

"*Are* you different? Really?"

"Of course I am. You saw me this afternoon. Before my birthday appointment with Gracie and Kim."

"Yes," he said. "I saw you. Before."

She didn't like his tone. Not at all. It seemed to say a lot more than his words did. She stated unequivocally, "I was never like Sara and Jenny."

And then she found herself wondering, *Or was I?*

When I was five. And my mother was still alive?

Was I like Sara and Jenny then? Talkative and friendly, sure that the world and everything in it was mine to enjoy and explore?

It was hard to remember. And maybe the truth was she didn't want to remember. It made her too sad to go back to those happy times.

Her mother had died when she was eight. That was when she first started to put on weight, after her mother died. It had been such a tough time. Not only had she lost her mother, but somehow it felt as if her father had gone away from her, too. Horace Taylor was lonely, just like Lynn was. He missed her mother so much.

And then he had met Jewel Hollis when Jewel hired on as a clerk at the family hardware store. Jewel had two daughters and her husband had left her.

When Horace had married Jewel, he'd adopted Trish and Arlene. They were all going to be a family, he had said. He and Jewel and their three daughters,

Arlene and Lynn and Trish. He had said that family was important, one of the most important things in life, more precious even than diamonds or gold.

Lynn had believed him. And from then on, her father hadn't seemed quite so lonely anymore. And Lynn had wanted them all to be happy.

She'd learned quickly that happiness in her new family could be achieved by doing what her stepmother wanted. By being the kind of daughter Jewel needed. Jewel already had two petite, pretty, popular girls. She needed someone she could count on. A dependable one.

Lynn had become that. The dependable one. Not popular or pretty, too tall and too plump. But reliable. Someone who helped Jewel with the meals and the dishes, someone willing to pick up after Arlene and Trish. Arlene and Trish, after all, didn't really have time for chores. Schoolwork was harder for them than it was for Lynn. And they wanted to spend their spare time with their friends.

"I'll bet you *were* pretty," Ross said. "When you were in kindergarten. I'll bet you were good in school and that you laughed and that sometimes your teacher had to ask you to quiet down."

Lynn smiled to herself, thinking of Sara, giggling so gaily—and promising to "zipper" her lip. "Maybe," she allowed. "But it was a long time ago—and how did we get off on this subject, anyway?"

"It was a natural progression—from your favorite students, to why they're your favorites."

"But we weren't even supposed to be talking about me."

"I was curious, that's all."

"Well. Is your curiosity satisfied?"

"As much as it's likely to be."

What did that mean? She felt it would be wiser not to ask. "Is there any more you need to know about Jenny?"

"No, I think you've about covered it. I wonder if you could write me up a brief report of what you've just told me? Only a page or two. To put in her file?"

"Sure. I'll get it to you in a day or two. Will that do?"

"That will be fine."

She glanced at the big clock on the fireplace mantel. As she did, a single chime rang out. Eight-thirty. She untucked her legs. "I should go."

He said nothing.

She bent down to pull on her shoes. When she straightened to a sitting position again, he was staring at her. She read the look in his eyes. And answered it as if he had actually spoken. "Ross. It *is* getting late."

"Eight-thirty isn't late."

"I won't be home until nine, at least. And it's a school night."

"So what? Live dangerously."

Live dangerously. She wished he hadn't said that. All at once those moments upstairs didn't seem long ago at all. They came back to her vividly, stealing her breath: the two of them, standing by that claw-footed table, his hands cradling her chin, his lips brushing, only once, so sweetly, against her own.

She ordered such thoughts away. "I think I've lived dangerously enough for one night."

He answered in a low voice, "No, you haven't. You've flirted with danger. And that's all."

"That's more than enough, I think," she told him tartly. "It's certainly more than I should have done."

"But less than you wanted to do."

Another sharp remark rose to her lips. She held it back.

Her silence seemed to anger him. "What? Say it." His eyes were very dark. She saw heat in them. The heat of desire. Her body responded instantly, going weak. Pliant. Yearning toward him...

"I have to go." She said it firmly. In a tone any one of her young students would have recognized. The tone that said she would not be pushed one inch further.

Ross got the message. "All right." He watched her through unreadable eyes as she stood.

"I'll just get my coat and my—"

He silenced her by rising himself, a swift, fierce movement, one that frightened and excited her at the same time.

"Don't—" she said, and that was all.

He reached out, caught her hand and pulled her close. "One kiss," he said.

His heat and strength surrounded her. She put her hands on his chest to push him away—and felt his heart beating under her palm. "Your heart," she heard herself whisper. "I can feel it...."

He said her name, so softly. "Lynn..."

In his eyes she saw promises. Promises she knew he didn't think he was making. Promises he probably *wasn't* making. Promises she only thought she saw. Because she dreamed the bright, hopeful dreams of the plain girl, the overweight, unpopular girl, the hardworking, quiet, *dependable* one...

She said flatly, "You know very well it won't just be one kiss."

"Do it anyway."

She stiffened her arms a little, to keep him at bay. "Don't you...*dare* me, Ross. Not about this. This isn't a bite of truffle cake we're talking about now."

His arms tightened around her. "Isn't it?"

"No, it is not."

His eyes seemed to reach down inside her, to grab hold of her in all her most private and forbidden places. He muttered, "Maybe you need to be dared. Maybe there's a woman inside you that you need to let out."

"That's my choice to make. Not yours to make for me."

Those words stopped him. "You're right," he said. "Get your things. We'll go." He released her and stepped away.

And all she wanted was for him to grab her close once more.

Oh, what was the matter with her? She was a plainspoken, direct person. She never said one thing and meant something else altogether.

Or at least, she never had until tonight.

"Go on," he said more gently. "Get your coat."

It was a long walk to that front closet. But she made it. She had the closet door open and was staring at her plain brown coat hanging there when the truth hit her.

She shut the closet door.

She heard his footsteps, coming closer. And then he was there, at her back. She could feel him, feel the very maleness of him. So close. Too close...

"Lynn." His voice was so tender, a caress of sound in her ear.

Her legs felt weak, her whole body trembled. She still had her hand on the knob.

She leaned into it, resting her forehead against the door. "I...don't want to go."

He didn't say anything. He didn't have to, really. She closed her eyes, pressed her head harder against the ungiving wood, let out a ragged breath. "Isn't that crazy?"

She waited. Still he said nothing.

And she couldn't bear to face him, not yet. Not until she'd thoroughly confessed her own foolishness. She whispered, "It's all wrong. And I'm scared. I've never...done anything like this before. I hardly know you. And I'm a *teacher*. A teacher is expected to behave a certain way. But..." She couldn't go on.

After a minute he took her arm. She stiffened in self-defense against his touch, against the real kindness in it that seemed to her to verge on something like pity.

She had liked it better when he dared her, she really, truly had.

He made a soothing sound. "Come on. Look at me."

Reluctantly she let go of the doorknob and turned. His hand slid down to clasp with hers. "Look at me. And listen. Are you listening?"

She bit her lip and nodded.

"I'm a damn good lawyer," he said.

She stifled a laugh, a laugh that felt a little too much like a sob. "What has that got to do with anything?"

"If you'll listen, I'll tell you."

"I...all right."

"I'm a damn good lawyer. But the truth is, I'm not a very good man."

She had an instant and rather powerful urge to argue with him—and he knew it.

With the hand that wasn't holding hers, he touched a finger to her lips. "Shh. Listen. I'm not a very good man. But you're one hell of a woman. And not just because of an appointment at the Whitehorn Salon and a pretty new dress. You've got heart and you've got guts. A sense of humor—and a damn sharp tongue. You're going to do fine. You're going to find yourself that prince you're looking for."

"But I—"

"Shh. Wait. Listen."

She pressed her lips together, nodded.

"That prince is not me. That prince was never me. Do you understand?"

She should have nodded again then. But she didn't. She couldn't. Deep in her most secret heart, she simply did not believe him.

You *are* my prince, her heart cried—at the same time as she called herself ten thousand kinds of fool.

He said, "All I want from you, and I admit, I want it pretty damn bad, is one night. I'm not looking for anything more than that. I'm no *good* for anything more than that. And you...I don't think you realize yet all that you are. But you will. As time goes on. And you'll be glad you never gave yourself away to someone like me." He paused, giving her a chance, she knew, to say something at last.

But she didn't say anything. She couldn't. She

only looked at him, all the reasons she had to leave now scrolling through her mind.

All the reasons that just didn't stack up against a night of magic. Against a lifetime of being the good girl, of saying and doing the right thing. Of wearing flat shoes and brown skirts, of having all the cowboys she'd gone to school with call her "Miss," defining her utterly with that single syllable: Miss. An old maid at twenty-four.

He had said it himself: *Maybe there's a woman inside you that you need to let out.*

Didn't he realize? That woman *was* out. She had been lured out, by her dear friend Danielle, by the tender ministrations of Gracie and Kim. By a silver-threaded red dress and two-inch red heels.

And by him. By Ross Garrison. By candlelight, over champagne and filet mignon, in a single bite of truffle cake delivered to her on the tip of his own fork.

That woman *was* out. And Lynn Taylor did not intend to hide her away again.

Not yet, anyway. Not until the night was over.

Not until she'd done all the forbidden things that the *dependable* one could never let herself do. Not until she'd squeezed every last drop of beauty and wonder out of all the moments until…when? Midnight. Yes. Of course. Midnight. She would stay until the clock struck twelve.

"Let's get that coat," he said, releasing her hand and reaching for the closet door.

She backed up, blocking the door. "One night?" she asked. "That's all, right?"

He closed his eyes, shook his head. "Lynn. I'm trying to do the right thing here, damn it."

She put her hand on the knob so he couldn't grab it. "One night," she said again. "Tonight."

He made a low, impatient and very put-upon sound. "Stop this."

"No. Sorry. I'm not going to stop. I assume you have…whatever single men are supposed to have. So that their lady friends don't end up in trouble."

He let out a harsh rush of air—like a man who'd been punched in the stomach. "You are not saying this."

"Yes, I am. Just tell me. Can you make sure that I don't get pregnant?"

He swore.

"Well, can you?"

"Damn it, yes. But—"

She put up a hand—the one that wasn't keeping him from opening the closet door and taking out her boring brown coat. "Listen, please. It's my turn to talk. And what I'm trying to tell you is that I want this one night as much—no, more. Definitely more than you do. I want you to—" she had to pause, to swallow, but then she did get the words out "—make love to me."

He swore again.

She hurried on before he could say more. "I want you to make love to me. I want you to show me…what it can be like. Because, you see, I really don't know. I want you to give me this one night, since that's all you say you're capable of. And then when it's over, I want you to keep your mouth shut about it. Do you think you can do that?"

"I don't believe you're saying this."

"You're repeating yourself."

"Damn it, Lynn. It's not right."

She clucked her tongue. "Listen to yourself. You sound like the good man you just told me you weren't."

"I am not a good man." He spoke through clenched teeth.

"If you say so. But you *do* want to make love with me?"

"What I want isn't the point."

"It's not?" Boldly she let her gaze travel downward, over his autumn-gold sweater and his fine leather belt. She could see the hard ridge that tented the fabric of his slacks—and she knew her biology, even lacking as she was in firsthand experience. She could see very clearly that her proposal had interested him.

He let out another low sound, this one more like a groan than anything else, and he muttered, "I should have had sense enough to keep my damn jacket on."

She looked into his face again—and her cool pose fell away. "I mean this," she said honestly. "I do want this. So much. And I give you my word, I won't ask you for anything more. After tonight, if we meet on the street, I promise to smile politely, say hello…and walk on by."

His eyes bored into her. "Walk on by?"

"Yes. Do you believe me?"

"Hell." It was all Ross could think of to say. He did believe her. And he should have been content. It was only everything he wanted, wasn't it? One night with her—and nothing more? Their little secret that neither would ever be so foolish as to share with anyone else.

She said very seriously, "I hope you believe me. Because I'm telling the truth."

A silence fell. A weighty one. She looked at him and he looked at her. The air seemed almost too thick for breathing.

Finally she asked in a thready voice, "Is this the part where I have to start begging?"

There was less than a foot between their bodies. He eliminated that distance, reaching for her as she reached for him.

He pulled her close, muttered into her hair, "Are you sure?"

She nodded against his shoulder, all doubts banished by the mere feel of his body pressed to hers, by the way his arms held her, contradicting utterly what he'd told her he wanted—one night and no more. Those arms really felt as if they'd never let her go.

"I'm sure," she whispered, not letting herself think of the lies she would have to tell, or of who she was: Jewel Hollis Taylor's dependable stepdaughter who would never, ever do such a shocking, wild thing.

Tonight. For this one night. She was someone else. Tonight, dependable Lynn Taylor didn't exist.

Tonight she was Cinderella. Sleeping Beauty. Ugly duckling turned swan.

And more.

Tonight she was…the lady in red.

She was the woman she'd seen in the mirror at the Whitehorn Salon. The woman who took her chances when they came along. The woman who dared to live dangerously. The woman who boldly said what she wanted and then went after it.

Tonight, just for this one night, a fairy-tale princess had nothing on her.

Chapter Six

He kissed her, right there in the front hall, pressing her up against the closet door. At first tenderly, gently, as if he feared hurting her.

And then she felt his tongue, questing for entry, at the seam of her closed lips. Slowly, only a little reluctantly, she opened for him. His tongue slipped inside.

Oh, my!

She could hardly believe it. A man's tongue, *Ross Garrison's tongue,* was inside her mouth.

And she...why, she *liked* it. It felt...slick and rough at the same time. And it was stroking her, caressing her, tasting faintly of brandy, of coffee and chocolate....

She opened her mouth a little more. And she moaned.

An answering sound, very male and very hungry,

came from deep in his chest. She could feel that sound. It made her shiver, made her breasts ache with a pleasant heaviness as it rumbled right through them, seeming to find its way straight to her heart.

His hand was sliding down to the small of her back, tucking her tightly into him. He…he was rubbing himself against her. Down there, she felt so warm. Like something solid held to flame and turning slowly liquid.

Omigoodness. Nothing in her life had ever felt quite like this. She'd read more than a few lush and lovely romances, curled up in her easy chair with a nice cup of tea. And sometimes, in the juicy parts, she'd let herself imagine that those passionate love scenes were happening to her.

But in real life? No way. Nothing had even come close. Certainly not that single quick peck on the lips she'd received at the door from one of those sweet, shy boys at Montana State.

She had definitely been missing out.

He kissed her harder, and his tongue delved deeper. Her legs went weak. She clutched at his broad shoulders, another moan escaping her, pressing her hips harder against him, wishing she could just melt right up into him, have her body be part of his body, softness and hardness blending together into one.

But then he lifted his mouth from hers. She stared up at him, wide-eyed. "I…you can keep going. It's all right, really…."

He frowned. "Are you *sure* that you're sure?"

"I said I was, didn't I?"

He chuckled, the sound low and seductively rough.

"You're right. You did say you were sure. But it still seemed like a good idea to check one more time."

She wrinkled her nose at him. "Okay, then. You checked. You don't have to check again."

"Whatever you say, Ms. Taylor."

She touched his mouth. It looked so soft and warm—and also a little bit swollen from the pressure of that kiss they'd just shared. His lips moved in a wordless caress against the tips of her fingers. She felt his breath flow down her palm.

He was tracing a slow, lazy circle at the small of her back. But then his hand strayed up. He touched her hair, capturing a curl, coiling it around his index finger.

She gave him a smile that quivered only a little. "So. What do we do now?"

He pulled his finger free of the curl he'd created. "We go upstairs."

"To…your bedroom?"

He nodded. And then, with a swiftness that stunned her, he put one arm at her back and one beneath her knees and lifted her high into his arms.

"Ross!" A wild laugh escaped her. "What are you doing?"

"What does it look like? I'm carrying you to my bed."

He turned without another word and started for the great room—and the wide, rough-hewn stairs. He strode up them purposefully, holding her close against his chest.

Halfway up, she lost one of her red shoes. The right one. It slipped off her heel. She tried to catch it on the end of her toe, but it got away from her. She heard it bouncing down behind them.

"Oh, wait!" she cried. "My shoe…"

"Leave it for now."

"But—"

"You can get it later. It's not going anywhere."

In his bedroom he set her gently on the bed, then knelt at her feet. She gazed dreamily down at his dark head as he removed her remaining shoe. "Ah," she said. "My prince."

Still kneeling there, cradling her left foot in his hands, he looked up at her. "I told you. I'm no prince."

She laughed. The sound was very naughty. She could do that tonight—give a naughty laugh, live dangerously. After all, for tonight, she was the lady in red.

Boldly she told him again, "You are my prince."

"No. I'm not."

"Yes, you are. But don't get nervous. No commitment required. Remember that old TV show, *Queen for a Day?*"

He lifted an eyebrow—and stroked the arch of her foot. "You're not old enough to remember *Queen for a Day.*"

She wiggled her toes at him. "There are such things as reruns, Ross."

He grunted. "Come on. They never reran *Queen for a Day*—not by the time you were growing up."

"Sure they did. I saw it when I was a little girl. It was a great show. Nice, middle-class housewives got to wear a crown and a fur cape with a long train. For a whole day, they were royalty. And there were prizes. Things like shopping sprees and brand-new washer/dryer combinations."

"And you're trying to tell me that this is the same thing?"

"It is. Very much the same. Only instead of a queen, you're a prince. *My* prince. For a night." She lifted her shoulders in a teasing shrug. "Sorry, I'm fresh out of washer/dryer combinations. All you get is me."

The news that he wouldn't get more didn't seem to worry him. He went right on stroking her foot, sending little heated shivers beneath her nylon stockings, little shivers that ran from her toes, along her arch, over the curve of her heel and right on up the back of her leg.

She hitched in a pleasured breath, then whispered, "Face it. You're the one. My Prince for a Night."

He raised her foot and lightly nipped her toe between his white teeth. A delicious weakness shivered through her. She had to rest back on her hands.

His palm cupped her heel. And then traveled, warm and encompassing, up the back of her calf to the tender spot behind her knee.

"All right." He said the words low, like a growl, from the back of his throat. A growl that sent her senses shimmering. "I'll be your Prince for a Night."

"Did I mention you don't get the cape or the crown, either?"

"No. But you did say the cape had fur trim—and a train, right?"

"Um-hmm."

"I think I can get by without that. And the crown…?"

"A diamond tiara, if I remember correctly."

"Do I look like a man who'd wear a diamond tiara?"

She tipped her head to the side, studying him. "Not your style, huh?"

"No, not my style."

"Well, good, then. It's settled. You get no crown, no cape, no prizes—except me. Temporarily."

"Do you hear me complaining?"

"Well, of course not. A prince *never* complains."

He didn't reply to that. Not in words. But his hand moved on, stroking beneath the silvered cashmere of her skirt, running up her thigh, eliciting a sharp gasp from her, and then sliding over, moving down the other thigh, appearing once more at her knee.

His head was bent again, watching what he touched. And then it came up. His eyes burned now, with a feral light.

He rose from a crouch to his knees. And then fully to his feet.

Still leaning back on her hands, she stared at him. He began to undress.

First he took off that platinum watch of his and set it on the stand by the bed. Then he pulled off his sweater and tossed it toward a chair, where it landed with a soft rustling sound. Next came the shirt he wore underneath it. He unbuttoned the sleeves with quick, almost brutal efficiency, then dispensed with the buttons that ran down the front. He shrugged out of the shirt and threw it toward the chair where his sweater lay.

He was naked from the waist up.

Without his shirt he seemed somehow too real.

Not her dream prince at all. But a man. A man she

didn't really know. A man who was going to do things to her that had never been done to her before.

Lynn realized that she didn't feel quite so naughty and free as she had a few seconds earlier.

His chest was…so broad and powerful, patterned lightly with dark hair that lay in a midnight shadow across his pectorals, then went down in a trail over his hard belly. Her gaze wandered lower. She saw that his…interest in this activity remained acute.

Her lips felt dry. She rubbed them together, dared to touch them with the moisture of her tongue.

He said one word low; she couldn't quite make it out, but it had a savage sound to it. A sound that matched the look in his eyes.

He held out his hand, palm out. A careful, controlled movement.

Lynn was a town girl, but she had grown up around men who worked with animals. She'd visited a few of the local ranches, gone to stock shows and rodeos. The way Ross reached for her now reminded her of the way a good cowhand will approach a skittish horse, every move cautious and deliberate, in order not to send it whinnying and wheeling away.

"Take my hand." It was a command, but couched in velvet.

Was she afraid of him right then?

Yes. Definitely. Afraid of the male power in him. Afraid of what she was about to do with him, which *could* bring great pleasure.

But which also could hurt her. Probably *would* hurt her, no matter how much care he exercised.

"Take it," he said.

Too late to back out now, she thought, sitting up straight again, extending her arm.

His fingers closed over hers. He pulled her slowly to her feet and then laid her hand on his chest. On that hardness, that heat. She felt the silky, slightly wiry hair, the expansion and contraction as he drew breath. And also the beating of his heart.

The beating of his heart.

The same as she'd felt it downstairs, when he'd kissed her, and even before that, when he'd dared her to let the woman inside her get free.

Well, here she was. Getting free.

She was also feeling more than a bit skittish.

And downstairs, the clock was chiming. The sound reached them. Neither spoke until all nine chimes had rung out.

Then he said, "We can still call a halt to this."

His eyes said something else altogether.

She didn't really know, at that moment, what he would do if she said, All right. Take me home. I've changed my mind.

And she would never know anyway, what he might have done.

Because she was not going to back out.

She closed her eyes, shook her head. "No. I want to stay, I do."

Beneath her hand, his chest contracted again as he released a long breath. "Good." He bent forward, nuzzled her mouth, then her cheek, then her temple, catching a few strands of hair between his lips and tugging on them gently.

She let out a long, shuddery sigh, her hand fisting of its own accord against his chest.

His naked chest.

Naked. The word got stuck in her mind, so scary and raw.

Naked.

In a few minutes, more than likely, he would expect her to start undressing, too. He would actually see her without her clothes on.

Would he like what he saw?

Lord, she hoped so.

After all, she *was* now slimmer than she used to be. Her stomach didn't pooch out—at least, not too much. And her breasts were…okay. There was really nothing wrong with them. Was there?

And her legs were long. That was one good thing about being tall. Long legs.

But still. Would she be…pretty enough?

Without her magical red dress?

Underneath, she was wearing a plain cotton slip. And her bra and panties…they were white. Boring and ordinary, as were her drugstore panty hose. Beneath the dress, everything belonged to the woman in brown.

Would he look at her and wonder why he'd wanted her to stay?

"Turn around," he whispered, his lips brushing her temple.

"I…what?"

"Just do it. Turn around."

"Oh. Oh, I don't know…."

"Do it. Turn around." He took her shoulders and slowly guided her so that she faced away from him. She found herself staring at the broad expanse of his bed. His hands slid down over her arms, then under them, to rest at the curve of her hips. "Better?"

Somehow, it was. Now, whatever he was looking at, she didn't have to know. She felt his hands move again—to the top of the zipper, beneath her hair, at her nape.

He smoothed her hair aside. And then he took that zipper down in an endless, nerve-flaying sizzle of sound. She felt the air against her back, and then his lips, at her nape, his breath against her skin.

She closed her eyes, suppressed a moan as he peeled the cashmere fully open, guided it over her shoulders and down. The top of the dress dropped away and he pushed it over her hips until it fell to the floor. She stepped free of it and he bent to pick it up.

She didn't dare look, but she knew that he turned. She heard him, felt the loss of his body heat as he moved away from her enough to lay the dress over a chair.

He came back. His hands were at her shoulders again, warm on her bare skin, lifting the straps of her slip and then dropping them, so they fell in twin loops down her arms.

His lips were at her ear. "Help me, Lynn. Just a little."

She responded to the tender command, sliding her arms free of the straps, then pushing the slip off her hips and shimmying it down, catching it in her hand, rising to her full height again—and tossing it toward where he'd laid her dress.

He made a sound of approval, low in his throat. And she felt his touch again, just a finger, at the base of her neck. He traced that finger downward, a slow glide along each of the bumps of her spine, pausing briefly at the back hooks of her bra. She held her breath. And then let it out as that finger continued on its way, stopping when it reached the elastic band at the top of her panty hose.

"Pretty," he whispered. "So soft…"

She smiled to herself. After all, he must be talking about her. About her skin. About her body. He certainly couldn't mean her everyday, unadorned underwear.

His steely forearm encircled her. He applied a gentle but definite pressure. She did moan then, as her body melted backward into his.

His hips cradled hers. He was still very much aroused. She could feel him, all along her back. She moaned again.

And he slipped his other arm around her, moving both hands up enough to cup her breasts. She looked down, saw his hands there, so tan against the plain cotton whiteness of her bra.

"Oh…" She sighed. "Oh, my…" She knew he could feel her hardened nipples, even through the bra. His thumbs were tracing them. "My oh my oh my…"

He chuckled in her ear, the sound as arousing as what his hands were doing to her breasts. He nuzzled her hair, then lower, putting his mouth on the side of her throat. She felt his tongue, moist and warm, tracing a circular pattern onto the tender skin of her neck.

Still holding her close with one encompassing arm, he used his free hand to take her bra straps down.

Seconds later, her bra was at her waist. And those hands of his cupped her naked breasts.

She let her head fall back against his shoulder. Her eyes drooped closed. "Tell me…I'm not doing this.…"

She felt his lips against her hair. "Sorry, Ms. Taylor. But you *are* doing this...."

He slipped one hand between them and with laudable dexterity unhooked her bra. It dropped away. She didn't even bother looking down to see where it fell.

As a matter of fact, she was not going to open her eyes. Not for a while, anyway.

This felt absolutely lovely. But things had moved so very far beyond dangerous. She wasn't taking any extra chances.

She kept her eyes closed.

His hands were roving again. The right one glided down over her stomach—and lower. She shuddered and gave another small, hungry cry as that hand slid between her thighs.

He was...cupping her.

She shuddered again. She could feel her own wetness—wondered wildly if *he* could feel it, even through the fabric of her panties and panty hose. With that cupping hand he pulled her up even tighter to him—was it possible that she could get any closer?

He whispered something soft in her ear. It might have been the word *yes*—or something else, something that wasn't really even a word at all. His cupping hand stroked her. She thought she just might faint.

And then at last he broke that intimate hold—to take her panties and panty hose away. He slipped slow, insistent fingers under both waistbands and then eased them down.

She helped him. Blindly, still not daring to look,

her hands meeting his hands, at her waist and then lower.

The nylon clung. Their hands kept brushing, fingers almost entwining, warm and eager and a little hurried now. Together, they managed to push the fabric down over her hips at last. She handled the rest of it herself, somehow getting it all down over her knees and her ankles, yanking her feet free, kicking the wad of stocking and panties aside.

She rose again, her eyes still shut, still with her back to him. He was waiting for her. His arms went around her, the muscles flexing, hard and so very warm. He went on caressing her, roaming her body freely now, over her breasts, down her belly—to the nest of curls below.

He touched her. There, in her most private place. And she had nothing, no last stitch of cotton or nylon, to protect her from that touch.

Gently he parted the curls, finding the slick, heated center of her.

And stroking.

Oh my oh my oh my oh my…

Did she cry those words aloud? Or were they only in her head? She couldn't tell. Couldn't separate one sensation, one sound from the other. His body was her body.

Everything was spinning magically, gloriously out of control.

Her legs couldn't hold her. She bent forward, found the bed to brace herself. He curved himself over her, not letting her go, his hand at the female heart of her, calling forth…

An explosion. A pulsing burst of purest sensation. She did cry out then, tossing her head back. Still he stroked her, till the pulsing took all of her, rushing out along every nerve ending, spilling through her whole body in a shower of heat and light.

She whimpered, stiffened. And went limp.

Gently he helped her to crawl onto the bed. She lay there on her side, her eyes still shut, feeling shattered and boneless, and he wrapped himself around her, spoon fashion, his bare chest against her back, his still-clad legs cradling hers.

Minutes passed. She didn't know how many. But he was so tender, just as a prince should be, stroking her arm, kissing her shoulder, touching her hair.

Finally he left her. She remained on her side, not daring to look as she felt the bed shift, felt him slide to the edge of it.

He was taking off the rest of his clothes. She heard his boots drop, one by one. The bed moved again as he got rid of his socks. And then yet again, as he stood. There was the whisking of his belt sliding free of its loops, and then more sounds: the slide of a zipper, the rustling of cloth.

She heard a drawer open—the one in the stand beside the bed. He took something out. Pushed the drawer shut. She heard a tiny tearing noise.

She closed her eyes even tighter. She might be totally lacking in experience. But she knew enough to realize he was taking the necessary precautions to protect her from pregnancy.

The bed gave once more. And he was back with her, wrapped around her again, as naked as she. His warmth felt so good. The hair on his legs scratched a little. And now…oh, now she felt his hardness quite intimately.

He grasped her shoulder. She didn't want to face him.

But she knew it was time to face him.

She let him turn her, so she lay on her back, though she couldn't stop herself from crossing her arms protectively over her breasts.

"Come on, Sleeping Beauty." He said it so low, so very softly. "Open your eyes."

She looked at him. He was smiling, just the kind of smile she needed right then, a smile that was careful and tender as his touch.

"All right?" he asked.

She nodded and kept looking at his mouth. She didn't quite dare to look into his eyes.

He rested his hand on her stomach and then moved it lower.

She stiffened.

He asked, "No?"

She gave a tiny whimper and another nod. "Yes," she said. "Honestly. Yes…"

So he touched her again, down where she was very wet now, threading his fingers through the bronze curls, finding the sensitive nub there and stroking it—until her arms forgot to protect her breasts and instead reached out for him. He lowered his dark head and tasted her bared breasts, kissing one and the other, drawing the aroused nipples into his mouth.

She pulled him closer as she felt her body rising again toward fulfillment, opening her legs wider, to give him better access.

He took what she offered, sliding fully on top of her, his big body crushing her a little as he positioned himself between her thighs.

She could feel him there, at her entrance. She gasped at the shock of it and stared into his face, seeking—what? Reassurance?

She found none. By then, he had none to give. He looked wild now, and primitive, poised there above her. All chance to stop, to go no further, utterly lost to her now.

He pushed in, a sure, firm flexing of his hips. It hurt. But not unbearably. Her tender inner muscles, relaxed by his attentions, gave to accommodate him.

He pushed again. And that time she cried out.

He lowered his mouth to hers, as if he could drink the pain from her lips, take it into himself and turn it to pleasure. He breathed her name; she parted her lips for him. His tongue delved in, hot and seeking.

Another deep thrust of his hips.

He filled her now.

She moaned into his mouth. He drank that sound, too, kissing her so hungrily, his hips pressed tight to hers below—tight and hard, but absolutely still.

Then, with a moan of his own, he dragged his mouth away. He buried his head in the curve of her shoulder.

And he began to move.

It really did hurt. It *burned.* She felt torn in two.

Still, she held on, lifting her legs and wrapping them around him, instinctively knowing that if she gave him her body fully, if she moved with him and didn't resist him, it would be better, not hurt quite so much.

And it didn't. Or rather, it did still hurt, but beneath the burning there was pleasure now.

A growing little glow of pleasure. She focused on

it, thinking of a tiny spark that only needed fuel and tending to burst into brightest flame.

He moved faster. And she tried to go with him. But his rhythm was so wild now, she couldn't quite keep up with it, couldn't make the magical little explosion come upon her again.

He stiffened, and she felt him, pulsing inside her. She clutched him closer still, her nails digging into his broad shoulders, her mouth making soft woman sounds as his climax rolled through him.

At last he went still, his full weight settling upon her, pressing her down.

She took his weight as she had taken his sensual invasion of her body, by relaxing into it. By not fighting it. She stroked her hands down his broad back, rubbed her cheek against his hair.

He whispered something sweet and apologetic, about being too fast.

But she only held him closer and softly commanded, "Shh..."

He smiled. She felt that, the movement of his lips against her throat. She sighed in real contentment.

Then, from downstairs, she heard a single chime. Nine-thirty.

"Don't listen to that," he muttered thickly. "It's still early...."

She said nothing, only moved her hands in long, slow caresses, up and down his back.

"That feels good," he said. "Don't stop."

"I won't."

"And don't get any ideas about leaving any time soon."

"Ross, did I say I wanted to leave any time soon?"

He chuckled. ''No, Ms. Taylor. I guess you didn't.''

She knew very well that she *should* leave. The later she stayed, the greater the chance that someone would find out just how she'd spent her birthday night.

But then again, tonight was all she had with Ross. And when tomorrow came...

Nope. Bad idea. Better not think about tomorrow.

This was now. This was tonight. There had been no night like it in her entire life. There would probably never be a night like it again.

And she refused to let it end until the clock struck twelve, at least.

Chapter Seven

They were in his bathtub when, far away downstairs, the clock struck ten. It was a very large bathtub, with massaging jets. Lynn lay back against Ross in the steamy bubbling water and they listened to the faint chimes.

"It's nothing." He made a trail of kisses, down from her temple, over her cheekbone, to her ear. "Ten o'clock," he whispered. "Nothing. Early." His hands cupped her breasts, which floated just near the surface, the nipples pointing pertly at the ceiling, the bubbling water covering them, then sliding away to reveal them with each pulse of those lovely massaging jets.

"Nothing." She sighed. "Ten o'clock is nothing...." With a sinuous flexing of her whole body, she rolled so she was facing him and braced her hands on his shoulders. She felt like a mermaid, a mermaid adrift in a hot, bubbly sea.

He hooked a hand around the back of her head and brought her mouth to his.

By ten-thirty they were back in his bed. The clock struck so distantly, sounding so far away. They smiled at each other. Only ten-thirty. They still had time.

By eleven they'd wandered downstairs to raid the refrigerator. He was feeding her vanilla bean ice cream straight from the carton. He held the spoon poised an inch from her mouth as the eleven chimes marked the hour.

When at last the clock was silent, he gave her the ice cream. And then he kissed her, urging her to open her mouth and share the treat with him.

She did.

And soon enough, both of them forgot all about what time it was.

Eleven-thirty?

That went by without Lynn even knowing it. They'd gone back upstairs. To the big bed. And the things that they did there were terribly distracting. If the clock did chime, Lynn certainly didn't notice it.

But she heard it at midnight.

She'd been dozing, drifting in and out of sleep, all wrapped up in Ross's arms. At the first faint, deeply melodious sound, she came fully awake.

She sat up, clutching the covers to her breasts, and counted off each chime, right up to the magic number.

Ross sat up beside her.

She turned to him. "Midnight." She felt…dazed. How could it be over so soon?

She shook herself and started to rise from the bed.

He grabbed her arm. "Time for my pop quiz." His voice sounded joking, totally offhand, yet his grip on her arm was anything but.

"Ross. I really can't stay any longer."

He gave up trying to tease her. "You can. For a while. For hours. We have hours yet."

"No. It's too dangerous. It really wouldn't be wise."

"To hell with 'wise.' Stay."

She could have resisted the command in his voice. But the plea in his eyes? How could she resist that?

"Stay," he said again.

"Not for too long…"

He muttered a low oath and pulled her against him.

Lynn woke to the distant sound of the clock striking.

She turned her head and looked at the clock by the phone on the nightstand.

Six o'clock.

It couldn't be.

But the room *was* growing light.

Oh, God.

She pressed her eyes shut again, but it didn't help. Memories from the night before assailed her. All the bold things she'd said. All the brazen, shocking things she had done. She had sipped brandy. She'd drunk champagne. She'd begged a man to make love with her.

And he had. Repeatedly.

Her eyes popped open again. Keeping them shut wasn't helping.

She turned her head slowly.

The man beside her lay on his stomach, his face turned away from her. The sheet was rumpled at his waist, revealing a broad expanse of muscular back.

Still asleep.

He was still asleep. And it was six o'clock in the morning. Dawn was breaking. She had to get out of there.

She sat up. Her heart was beating so fast it scared her. Adrenaline raced through her system.

Think, she commanded her panicked mind. Think logically.

But she just couldn't stand to think. Not right then. If she started thinking, she'd only realize what an awful mess she'd gotten herself into.

She'd only start picturing his face, what it might look like—when he opened his eyes and saw her in his bed in the harsh light of day. Maybe he'd look at her tenderly.

Then again, what if he didn't? What if he looked at her as if he wished she wasn't there?

She recalled what he'd said last night.

All I want from you is one night. I'm not looking for anything more than that.

No. Better not wake him.

Better...what?

Get up. Get out of there. Just get up and get out.

Willing him not to stir, she slid from the bed and rushed around on tiptoe, grabbing for her scattered clothes. Her dress, slip and bra lay across a chair, her panties and panty hose in a knot on the floor. And her shoes...

Well, there was one of them, right by the bed. She snatched it up. The other was…where? She remembered. It was somewhere on the stairs.

She fled across the hardwood floor, past the sitting area with its big leather chairs, over the beautiful kilim rugs. The door was open. They'd never bothered to pull it closed when they came back up the stairs from their visit to the kitchen—where the clock had struck eleven as he was feeding her a bite of ice cream.

Memory stunned her again: the cold, creamy sweetness melting on her tongue. And then his kiss…

No. It was not a time to think of kisses.

It was morning now.

And she had to go.

She went through the door, rushed along the hall and paused at the top of the stairs to struggle awkwardly into her clothes. The panty hose were torn. And she didn't want to waste time wiggling into them anyway. She dropped them on the floor as she yanked on her panties, put on her bra, her slip and the dress. She had to fight with the zipper a little, but she got it most of the way up. She grabbed the panty hose again, knowing she needn't have bothered. They were ruined. But she simply couldn't bear to just leave them there, for him to find.

With the wad of panty hose in one hand and the shoe in the other, she ran down the stairs, looking wildly for that other shoe.

Where was it? She distinctly recalled the moment it had dropped from her foot. It had to be here somewhere. She got all the way to the bottom and looked around on the floor there. Nothing. She turned and sprinted halfway up again. But no. It really wasn't there.

And what was that? A noise, from upstairs?

Was he awake? Would he leave his room and find her here, running up and down the stairs, rumpled and frantic, looking for her silly shoe?

Forget it. Just forget it.

Forget it and get out.

She dashed for the front hall and the closet there. Yanking open the door, she ripped her coat from the hanger, which banged around on the rod and then clattered to the floor. She tried to catch it—and then let it fall. So silly. What did it matter if she left a hanger on the floor?

She shoved her arms into the sleeves of her coat, scooped up her purse and stuffed the panty hose inside it. The hanger wedged itself in the closet door when she tried to shut it.

Fine. She left it open.

She whirled, clutching her purse and her single shoe, and raced for the front door.

The latch gave with a heavy click. He had never locked it. She pulled the door open, paused briefly to shut it behind her, and ran out into the cold autumn morning.

The rough deck boards were icy under her naked soles. She tried to ignore the chill as she fled down the wide steps and onto the front drive, which was lined with tall, proud evergreens.

The trees gave way to open land about halfway to the road. And the pavement ended, too. The rest of the driveway was hard-packed dirt. Dirt and sharp pebbles that dug into the tender skin of her soles.

She kept running, the chill morning air rushing

hard in and out of her lungs. She could see the two-lane road, Route 17, where the drive met it, not two hundred yards away.

What would she do when she got there?

Flag someone down?

A stranger?

No. She'd never have that kind of luck.

The odds were that, if anyone did come along, she would know them. And they would know her. Some cowboy from one of the local ranches. Someone driving into town to run errands, to enjoy an early breakfast at the Hip Hop Café.

And wouldn't that someone have a tale to tell over his biscuits and gravy?

"Picked up Horace Taylor's girl, the kindergarten teacher, this mornin'. Out on Route 17. Barefoot, and lookin' wild as a corn-crib rat. Like she'd been out all night. Yep. Strayed off the main trail, that's for certain...."

Oh, she could just hear the tongues starting to wag.

Once Lily Mae Wheeler got the news, it would be over.

"Well, I do not like to carry tales. But I have to say I saw her last night, sipping champagne at the State Street Grill. With that lawyer, Ross Garrison. I guess we don't have to wonder where they went next. We all know that new house of his is out on Black Bear Lake. And that the way to Black Bear Lake is on Route 17. And honey, here in Whitehorn, we also know what you get when you add two and two...."

But no. That wasn't fair to Lily Mae. Lily Mae wouldn't sound like that. She wouldn't judge Lynn. She did have a good heart. But she would talk. Her words would be kinder, but they'd say the same things.

And there would be others ready, willing and able to judge.

Because in Whitehorn they not only knew how to add two and two. They also expected their school-teachers to keep to the main trail.

Oh, God, maybe she should have thought a little harder, after all, before she'd grabbed up her clothes and fled the bedroom and the man sleeping there.

Her feet slowed.

She clutched the collar of her coat at the neck and looked around her.

The wind had died during the night. The still air smelled of pine. Overhead, a hawk wheeled through the endless sky. Off to the northwest, the twin peaks of the Crazies rose up, craggy and tipped in white, the shadow of one dark across the other as the sun sent a wash of golden light from its rising place in the east.

A slight dusting of frost lay crisp and sparkling over the yellowed grass. Barbed-wire fences stretched on either side of the drive. Cattle, mostly black-baldies, but some Herefords as well, grazed beyond those fences. They lipped up grass, then chewed away patiently, raising their big heads and turning to watch her through eyes that appeared both utterly empty and infinitely wise.

Whose cattle, Lynn wondered, in a pointless effort to distract herself from the absurdity of her predicament. What ranchers grazed their herds out here, along Route 17, by Black Bear Lake?

She didn't know, offhand.

And it didn't matter anyway.

What mattered was that she would have to go back.

Go back and wake him, if he hadn't awakened already.

Go back and ask him to please take her to her Blazer, which still waited in the parking lot at her school.

Her feet dragging now, Lynn reached the two-lane road. She stopped on the cowcatcher, a wide grate across the drive that kept cattle from straying. The air beneath the grate seemed even colder than the ground.

Oh, her poor feet. Covered with dust and aching with cold. And cut up a little bit, too. They'd be in even worse shape by the time she limped back to the house.

But what else could she do? She never should have lost her head and run off on her own in the first place.

And what was that sound?

The hum of an engine. Someone was coming. It looked like a pickup, but it was still too far up the road to be sure.

Lynn whipped her head to the left and right, shamelessly seeking someplace to hide.

There was nothing. Just open land and barbed wire and grazing cattle. A single spindly-looking pine stood about twenty feet away. No time to reach it, though, before the vehicle went past. And what kind of cover could it provide anyway? The branches were too thin, the trunk way too narrow. She'd only look like the guilty ninny that she was, trying to crouch behind it.

The engine of the approaching vehicle roared

louder. Closing in. There was little doubt now that the driver would have spotted her.

She had two choices. She could take off at a run back the way she had come and pray that whoever it was had failed to recognize her—in which case, he'd probably decided she must be some crazy woman, stranded alone out here, someone who needed help.

That would mean he would come after her.

Oh, that would be lovely.

So she could run—and probably get caught anyway.

Or she could stay and face the music.

Her whole body was shaking, with humiliation more than cold.

She gritted her teeth and commanded the shaking to stop. Miraculously, it did. Drawing back her shoulders, she sucked in a quivering breath and looked up the road.

The battered pickup trundling her way was close enough now that she recognized it. It belonged to Winona Cobbs, the woman most people in White-horn believed to be a psychic. Winona Cobbs, probably headed into town to pick up a few things.

And doubtless to have breakfast at the Hip Hop Café with her friend Lily Mae.

Chapter Eight

The old pickup crossed the broken line that ran down the center of the road and rattled to a stop right next to where Lynn stood on the cowcatcher. The woman in the driver's seat, her gray hair braided and coiled into a crown on top of her head, stared at Lynn through the side window with fathomless eyes.

Lynn stared right back.

After a minute, Winona cranked the window down. "Good morning, Lynn." The wrinkles that spread like fans from the corners of those wise eyes deepened as she smiled. "It's a little cold this morning."

Lynn fisted her hand a bit tighter at her coat collar. "Yes. It is. Very brisk."

"Looks like you forgot to wear your shoes."

It was only a simple observation on Winona's part. It shouldn't have inspired a flood of emotion. Still,

Lynn felt a hot, insistent pressure at the back of her throat.

No. She would not.

She would not surrender to the final humiliation of bursting into tears. She gulped those tears, swallowed them back down her throat. Then she held up her remaining shoe and spoke with as much dignity as she could muster. "I didn't forget to wear my shoes. I've lost one, that's all."

"Hmm," said the psychic. "Hmmm…"

Lynn didn't like the sudden faraway look in Winona's eyes. "Er…Winona?"

The older woman poked a plump hand out the open window. She wore a huge squash-blossom ring on her third finger. "Give me that."

Reflexively, Lynn grabbed her shoe close. "What?"

"Give me that shoe."

"I don't—"

"The shoe. Let me have it."

"But—"

Winona snapped her fingers. "Give it to me. Now."

Something in Winona's voice made Lynn hold out the shoe. Winona took it. Lynn felt it leave her hand and longed to reach in the window and snatch it back.

But it was too late. Winona clutched the shoe to her generous bosom and closed her eyes. A humming sound issued from deep in her chest.

Lynn suggested sheepishly, "You know, Winona, I don't really think I'm in the mood for a vision right now."

Winona was not listening. She began speaking

low, in an eerie singsong. "What is lost shall be found, in a scattering of dust...."

Lynn cleared her throat. "Winona, I mean it. It's just...not a good time for me."

Winona didn't seem to care what time it was. She still had her eyes closed. She was swaying a little in her seat now, her head facing front, cradling Lynn's shoe as if it were a lost, needy child.

"Winona. Can you hear me?"

"A ring and a lie," Winona chanted. "A lie that brings truth..."

"Winona. Please..."

"The teacher teaches, the prince must learn...."

The prince...

Lynn let out a small cry as last night came spinning back to her again, stunning and lovely. Utterly wrong. Terrifyingly right...

"They shall take the wrong twin. But love shall return, in the darkest night of fear and misery...and silence. I do hear the silence. Such a horrible silence, when the lost one comes home...." Winona turned her head slowly. She opened her eyes and looked right at Lynn, right *through* Lynn, it felt like. Her wrinkled mouth bloomed in a smile full of secrets, of mysteries, of the limitless unknown.

Lynn felt the goose bumps, rising all over her body, goose bumps that had nothing at all to do with the morning chill.

"Only remember..." Winona's voice was a sigh. It was the wind, blowing down off the Crazies, rustling the pine trees, making the branches whisper together. "Through it all, there is but one magic. And that magic is love. Believe in it. It won't let you down. Do you hear me, child?"

"I…yes." Lynn's reply felt dragged out of her. "Yes, I hear you. I do."

The secret smile faded. Winona blinked and shook her head. "Well. That was interesting." Her wild gray eyebrows drew together. "Did you get anything from that?"

Lynn had no answer ready. At that moment, she could only stare.

"Never mind," Winona said gently. "When the time is right, all will be revealed—and you had better hop in, don't you think?"

The swift change of subject made Lynn stagger back a step.

"Come on, come on…." Winona leaned away from Lynn to open the passenger door.

Still, Lynn hesitated, the strange things Winona had said whirling through her mind.

A ring and a lie?

And what twin? There were no twins in Lynn's life right now. Were there?

"Are you coming with me or not?" demanded Winona.

"Yes. Yes, I'm coming." It seemed the most logical course at that point. She'd already been caught. And going with Winona would save her poor feet the painful walk back to that house, save her from having to see Ross, to talk to him, to look into his eyes.

"Hurry up, then."

"Yes. All right." Lynn ran around the front of the pickup and climbed in.

"Shut that door now. I'll turn up the heater." Winona clucked her tongue. "Just look at those feet of yours."

"They'll be all right. Really."

"Here."

Lynn accepted her shoe.

Winona flipped a dial and a strong blast of warm air issued from under the dashboard. "How's that?"

"Wonderful. Thank you."

"You want to go home?"

"No. Take me to my school, please."

Winona shifted into gear and steered the old pickup back out onto her side of the road.

It was seven o'clock when Lynn parked her Blazer in the driveway of the clapboard-sided house on Shiloh Street where she had grown up.

She had exactly one hour to pull herself together, drive back to the school and be ready at her desk when the eight-o'clock bell rang.

She was terribly tempted to call in sick, to run to her bedroom, jump into her bed and hide there until—when?

No. It wouldn't work. Winona was probably at the Hip Hop right now. Comparing notes with Lily Mae. Adding two and two and coming up with four. Lynn's fall from grace would be all over town by lunchtime. If she cowered in her bedroom, she would only make an awful situation worse. She might be labeled a fallen woman by some. But she would be a fallen woman who kept her back straight and her chin high, thank you very much.

Her purse and her shoe were lying on the seat. Lynn picked them up and got out of the Blazer, her mind turning to thoughts of her sister, who would be waiting inside.

Pretty, petite Trish, Lynn thought bleakly. Trish, with her big crush on Ross Garrison. Trish, who was going to be hopping mad at Lynn when word of where Lynn had been last night got around. Trish, who would end up feeling hurt and betrayed...

Lynn wanted to beat herself over the head with her red shoe. What had ever made her imagine that she would get away with this?

The lady in red had stolen her one night of love.

And now the woman in brown would have to pay the price.

Shamefully, Lynn couldn't keep herself from trying to enlist the sympathy of the Almighty as she limped up the front step.

Please, dear God. I know I've done wrong. But let Trish still be in bed. Let me be able to put off facing her for just a little bit longer. Just do this one thing for me, oh, won't You please?

God did not answer her cowardly prayer.

When Lynn let herself in the door, Trish was standing in the tiny front foyer, fully dressed in a tight denim skirt and satiny blouse. Her small, slim hands were fisted on her hips. She tossed her head of shining black hair and began firing off angry questions.

"What's going on? Where have you been? How could you scare us like this?"

"Trish, I..."

But the recriminations had started. And Trish ran right over Lynn in her eagerness to let them all out. "You've been gone all night and you never stayed out past ten in your whole life. I have been just about out of my mind. Mom called. To wish you a happy birthday. That was at about seven last night. I told her I'd have you call her when you got in. But you didn't get in. And then, around ten, she called again.

When I said you still weren't here, she got all frantic. You know she's not supposed to let herself get frantic. You know it's not good for her heart.'' Jewel had suffered a mild heart attack not long after Lynn's father had died. Her doctor was constantly reminding her to take her medication—and not to let herself get worked up about things.

Trish barreled on. ''But she *was* frantic. And then *I* started getting frantic. I called that friend of yours, that Danielle Mitchell, and she said I shouldn't worry. She said she was sure that you were just fine.''

Trish tossed her head again and huffed out an outraged breath. ''Just fine, that's what she told me. That's *all* she would tell me. So I had to call Mom back and try to settle her down. It wasn't any picnic. She wanted to call the sheriff's office, and it took just about all the convincing I had in me to keep her from doing it. When I finally got off the phone with her, I went to bed. But I didn't sleep hardly a wink and—'' Trish cut herself off in midtirade, her jade-green eyes narrowing.

Lynn looked down. Her coat had fallen open.

Trish had seen what was underneath. ''Where did that dress come from? And what did you do to your hair—and why are you running around barefooted?''

''Trish,'' Lynn began, and then had no idea what to say next.

''Trish?'' her sister repeated. ''*Trish?* Is that all you've got say to me? Just my own name?''

''I...I'm running very late. I have to get to my classroom.''

Trish marched to the foot of the stairs and planted

herself there, blocking Lynn from going up them. "I want to know where you've been all night long."

"No, you don't," Lynn muttered under her breath.

"What? What was that?"

Lynn drew herself up. It seemed she'd had to do that a hundred times already since daybreak. Suck in a breath and set her chin high. "Listen. I'm very sorry if I frightened you. It was terribly thoughtless of me not to call you."

"Humph. Well. It sure was."

"Please...forgive me. I'll never do that again." She meant that. With all her heart. Once, after all, was stacking up to be way more than enough.

"But where *were* you?"

"I just...don't have time to go into it now. I have to get to work. I really do."

Trish folded her arms across her chest and looked truculent. "I just want to know what is going on here."

"There is nothing going on." Was that a whopping lie, or what? But what else could she say? She had neither the time nor the heart to tell Trish the grim truth right now.

And maybe, deep in her coward's soul, she was still hoping that she wouldn't have to. That Lily Mae and Winona would never get around to comparing notes, to adding two and two.

"Trish, please. We can discuss this tonight. But now I've got to get ready for work."

Trish tapped her dainty foot and made a tight, growling sound. "Oh, all right. Fine. You just go on. You get ready for work." She moved to the side a fraction.

Lynn saw her chance and took it. She slid around her sister and hurried up the stairs.

Thirty minutes later she was rushing back down. She got out the door before Trish could appear again and start asking more questions.

She'd reached her Blazer when she saw the Mercedes SUV, parked on the street not twenty feet away.

Ross.

Just sitting there, in the driver's seat, looking at her.

Well, and what was he supposed to do, a voice in her mind inquired dryly, the way you ran off like that, miles from town on foot? The man might not be looking for a permanent relationship, but he'd certainly want to be sure that his lady friends got home all right.

She ran to his driver's side window before he could decide to get out and come to her.

He pushed a button and the window slid down.

She started talking before he could say anything. "I'm fine. I'm sorry if I scared you. As you can see, I got home all right."

"Did you?" His voice sounded...she couldn't really say how it sounded. Distant. Wary. A little bit cold.

She looked at his side view mirror. At her neighbor's curtained windows opposite where he'd parked. She couldn't bear to look directly at him. And Lord, how she hoped no one had seen him.

"Yes, it all...worked out. You didn't happen to bring my shoe, did you?"

"Your shoe?"

She could tell from the tone of his voice that he didn't know what she was talking about. "The one that fell off my foot. On the stairs? I couldn't find it this morning."

"I haven't seen it. I'll look for it, though."

"Good. All right. And I'm late. I have to go."

"Lynn—"

A whimper of pure misery escaped her. "Just…please. I really do have to go. Don't worry about me. I'm fine. I'm just fine."

Before he could say another word, she turned and left him, praying he wouldn't be foolish enough to get out and come after her.

He wasn't. She heard the Mercedes start up. She was getting into her Blazer when he pulled away from the curb and drove off.

Somehow, Lynn got through the morning at school. She did her job and she thought she did it reasonably well.

Danielle arrived to pick up Sara a few minutes after everyone else had left. She had Lynn's plain skirt and blouse folded over her arm—and a worried look in her eye.

She spoke to her daughter first. "Go and get your things, Sara, and put on your jacket."

Once Sara had disappeared into the coat nook, Danielle turned to Lynn. "Trish called me last night."

"I know. She told me."

"Are you…okay?"

Lynn looked into her friend's eyes. She saw understanding and affection there. And she knew that when she was ready to talk about this, there would be someone to listen. "I've been better. Have you…heard anything? Around town?"

"Heard anything?"

"Rumors. About me. And Ross Garrison…"

"No, not a word."

"Well. It's early yet."

Danielle sighed. "This doesn't sound good."

"It's not. I've been…really stupid. And thoughtless. And…actually, I think I hate myself right now."

Danielle squeezed her arm. "Come on, it can't be that bad."

"It's bad enough. Believe me."

Sara appeared in the doorway to the coat nook. "Mommy! I can't find my snack box."

"Keep looking."

"But I—"

"Sara. I'll be right there."

With a little grunt of irritation, Sara vanished again.

"Come to my place," Danielle said. "Tonight. After Sara goes to bed. We can talk then."

Lynn thought of Trish's angry green eyes. "I think I could end up being real busy tonight."

"When you're ready, then. My door is open."

"Thank you. It means a lot."

Lynn stayed in her classroom until five. She rearranged supply closets and cleaned out her desk, worked on her lesson plans and made turkeys and Pilgrim hats out of construction paper as examples for class projects, since the Thanksgiving season was coming up soon.

She found some crackers and a little box of raisins

in a desk drawer and ate them as the lunch she hadn't had time to pack.

She was hiding, and she knew it. Putting off facing people—her sister and the rest of her family, especially. But it was legitimate hiding, she rationalized. Because it was all work that really did have to be done.

The janitor came in at four to empty the wastebaskets. Lynn greeted him and he grunted a hello at her. Nothing out of the ordinary there.

The school secretary, Mrs. Parchly, stuck her head in the door at four-thirty. "My. You're working late...." Was that a knowing gleam in those slightly bulging eyes of hers?

"I...had a few things to catch up on."

"I brought you those new attendance forms."

Lynn took the forms and thanked her, then Mrs. Parchly left.

Lynn decided to stop at the market on her way home. It was only more avoidance of Trish and the bleak confrontation that waited at home, and she knew it. But she went anyway.

She thought that the checker looked at her strangely, but maybe that was just her own guilt and nerves talking. She saw several people she knew and all of them smiled at her and greeted her kindly.

She got home at six.

And found her stepmother's car parked in the driveway.

They were waiting for her in the kitchen, sitting at the round maple table in the breakfast nook: the women of her family. Trish and Arlene. And Jewel.

She stepped into the room with her two bags of

groceries and longed only to drop them and run. Run and run and never look back.

They knew.

She could see it on their faces. She had to force her legs to carry her the few steps to the counter opposite the stove. She slid the bags onto it.

Jewel spoke first. "Well," she said, her small pink mouth as tight as the string on a miser's purse. "You finally decided to come home and face us."

It went downhill from there.

Jewel had her accusations ready. "You just weren't satisfied, were you? Taking my house just wasn't enough for you."

Lynn bit back a defensive retort.

The house had belonged to Lynn's mother, and Lynn's father had left it to her when he died. He'd been fair. Fair about everything. He'd left the house to Lynn and the hardware store, since sold, to Jewel—and generous cash bequests to both Arlene and Trish.

But what good would it do to point that out now? The issue of the house was old ground. After the house became Lynn's, Jewel had moved in with Arlene and Arlene's husband, Clyde, and their children. But Jewel had refused to really let go of the house she still considered hers. They'd had more than one family conference about it, with Lynn's stepmother and her stepsisters acting resentful and injured, as if she'd stolen something from them. And with Lynn unwilling to give in and put their names on the deed with hers, but still trying to placate them, to make them see that she loved them and her father had loved them and they all ought to just let it be and go on.

Jewel wasn't letting anything be. She shook her head. "Oh, no. Taking my house wasn't enough. Scaring me to death last night, worrying over you, aggravating my heart condition, that wasn't enough, either. You had to steal Trish's lawyer, too. You're a snake in the grass, that's what you are."

Trish started wailing then. "We *trusted* you," she cried. "We *counted* on you. And look what you've done. Look how you've treated us. I found out at lunch. At the Hip Hop. Everyone is talking. Everyone knows what you did. And when I went back to work and tried to tell Ross how shocked I was about it, he looked at me with that cold, mean look he can get and he said it was none of my business. He said he'd asked you to *marry* him, and you had said yes. He said you're his *fiancée!*"

Lynn knew she must not have heard Trish right. "What? His...fiancée? He said—?"

"You heard me. You know you heard me. And don't try to act surprised. Ross Garrison *proposed* to you. Like you could forget that. Like it could just slip your mind that he asked and you said yes."

"He didn't—"

"Don't you do that. Don't you go playing innocent on top of everything else. Oh, how could you do this to me? To *me?* You knew that Ross Garrison was supposed to be mine!" Trish let out a long, passionate cry. Then she folded her arms on the table and buried her head in them. Her sobs filled the room.

Lynn stared at her sister's shaking shoulders and wondered if perhaps Ross Garrison had gone mad. They had talked about a lot of things last night, but marriage hadn't been among them. Why in the world would he have told Trish such a lie?

Arlene, who was six months pregnant with her third child, reached over the mound of her own stomach to stroke Trish's black hair. "Now, now, baby. Calm yourself. Calm yourself, now." She looked up at Lynn and a snarl curved her pretty lips. "Look what you've done to her. You're just…trash, that's what you are."

Trash. The ugly word echoed in Lynn's brain.

And Arlene wasn't finished. "We should have known, the way you started losing all that weight. We should have known that now you had the house and your teaching credential and your job at the school, you wouldn't need us anymore. You'd be ready to show your true colors at last."

Lynn couldn't let that pass. "That's not so. You're my family and I—"

Jewel was the one snarling now. "Your family. Hah. What you did a person doesn't do to her family. You have treated us like we were dirt."

Trish's head shot up. "That's right. Leenie and Mom are right. You always acted so good and pure, like you didn't even care that you were too tall and too fat and no boys ever asked you out. But we know the truth about you now. We know how you really are. And I won't stay in the same house with someone like you. I'm moving in with Mom and Arlene and Clyde and the kids. I have packed some of my stuff and it's in the car already. I'll come back for my other things later, sometime when you're not home."

The three tiny, furious women stood as one. "And I've quit that stupid job, too," Trish announced with a defiant shake of her head. "I can't stand to see Ross Garrison ever again in my life."

Three sets of green eyes glared at Lynn.

Then Jewel said, "Well. Do you have anything to say for yourself?"

Lynn scoured her mind. She could not think of a thing.

"Well," huffed Jewel. "I guess there's nothing you *can* say." She turned to her two daughters. "Come on, then. Let's go."

Lynn waited until she heard the door slam behind them. Then she carefully pulled out a chair and lowered herself into it. She sat there for a good ten minutes, staring blindly at the cheerful yellow café curtains that draped the breakfast-nook windows, wondering if her stepmother and stepsisters would ever speak to her again. And also wondering in a vaguely defiant sort of way why she should care if they did.

Eventually, Lynn pushed herself to her feet and went to the counter to put her groceries away. She had just emptied the second bag and was carefully folding it to save for reuse when the doorbell rang.

Lynn let out a long, tired sigh. She didn't want to talk to anyone else. Not tonight. She wanted to fix something simple, eat it and climb the stairs to a hot bath and the welcoming warmth of her own bed.

But the bell rang again.

"Just let it be a salesman," she muttered under her breath as she trudged to the front hall. "Someone to whom I can just say 'No, thanks,' and then shut the door."

But it wasn't a salesman.

It was Ross Garrison. He said, "We have to talk."

Chapter Nine

She'd managed not to look directly at him that morning, in front of the house. But now she couldn't stop herself.

He was wearing a different jacket than last night, this one of butter-soft leather. A different jacket. A different shirt and sweater, different slacks and different boots. Same watch, though.

And the same dark, knowing eyes.

Eyes she really did not want to meet.

But she was meeting them.

And in them she saw…the night before. All of it. Every last tender word and sweet, erotic caress.

"I looked all over. I couldn't find that shoe of yours."

"It's all right." Was that all he wanted to tell her? Well, fine. He had told her. She could shut the door.

She started to do that, but he put out a hand and stopped it from closing. "Let me in."

"Ross, I really don't think we need to—"

"We need to. Let me in."

"I don't want any more trouble. My family has just walked out on me. I've had enough for one night."

"God." He gripped the door tightly enough that his knuckles shone white. "I'm sorry."

"It's not your problem. Honestly." She gave the door another push.

But he kept the pressure steady. The door didn't move. "Look. I won't give you any trouble. I just want to talk."

"Talk?"

"Yes. Talk. And that's all."

Reluctantly she led him to the living room and gestured toward the sofa. But he didn't take a seat. He stood across the flowered rug from her and looked at her long and hard.

Maybe he was still upset about the way she'd run off that morning. She apologized again. "I'm sorry about this morning. I truly am. It was…really stupid of me, to take off like that. I lost my head. Then, by the time I came to my senses, Winona Cobbs came along." She thought of the older woman, clutching the red shoe and humming, chanting strange, disjointed things.…

Lynn shook her head to banish the uncomfortable memory. "I hitched a ride with her."

"And you're…all right?"

"Yes. I am." It took considerable effort, but she managed to inject a modicum of sincerity into the words. "I'm exhausted and…what? Depressed, I guess, in a numb sort of way. But I'll get over it. I really will.''

''I should have taken you home, at midnight, when you wanted to go.''

She waved a hand. ''Let's not go into all that. Please. Last night was…last night. It happened. It's over. We can't go back and fix what we did wrong.''

''Maybe we can. To an extent, anyway.''

That made no sense. The damage was done. She waited for him to explain himself. But he only stuck his hands into his pockets and looked down at the rug, as if it suddenly required his intense scrutiny.

She prompted, ''Ross?''

He lifted his head. ''I told your sister that I'd asked you to marry me. And that you had accepted my proposal.''

''I know. She told me. I couldn't believe you would have said something so insane as that.''

''Well, I did. It just slipped out.''

Anger rose inside her, hot and prickly, making her voice tart. ''Oh, come on. You are not the kind of man from whom things just slip out.''

Ross had no trouble picking up her hostility. And he couldn't blame her for it.

But the lie about their engagement really hadn't been anything he'd consciously planned to say. That damn Trish had been ranting at him. And he'd been thinking of Lynn. Worrying about her. Hating himself for taking advantage of her, a self-loathing made even more intense by the realization that last night hadn't been enough for him. He'd seduced an innocent. *Kept on* seducing her, all night long. He'd done enough to her. A lot more than enough.

Yet he couldn't stop himself from wanting to do it again.

And the way she'd run off really had scared him, reminded him too much of what had happened to his wife.

Elana had hardly been an innocent. But he *had* taken advantage of her. He had used her to get what he wanted. And when *she* had run off, stormed out of their house in a final hot rage, there hadn't been any sweet, old Mrs. Cobbs to come to her rescue.

Lynn was glaring at him. He ordered the bleak memories of Elana from his mind. "Your sister was yelling at me. Accusing me. Accusing you. Calling what happened a one-night stand. And I…just said it. I told her it wasn't a one-night stand, that I'd asked you to marry me and you had agreed."

Lynn's anger drained away. She felt weary again. And her feet were still sore from the abuse they'd taken during her silly flight down the long driveway that morning.

A pair of wing chairs flanked the coffee table. She edged over to one and sat down. "Well. I guess it really doesn't matter what you said. It's just one more outrageous rumor that will have to make the rounds."

"Maybe. But then again, maybe not."

She let her spine slump back in the chair. "Ross. I'm too tired to play word games. What are you getting at?"

He took a step toward her. "I've been thinking, that's all. Thinking that maybe we ought to just go along with what I said."

She wasn't slumping anymore. She was sitting up straight. And her heart had just done a forward roll.

Silly, silly heart, she thought. What's the matter with you? "Go along?"

"Yes. Pretend that we really are engaged."

Her heart settled down again as she picked up on the operative word. "Pretend?"

"That's what I said."

"But what good will that do?"

"A lot. Think about it. What are you worried about—besides your sister finding out, which she already has? You're worried about the fact that you're a teacher. That you're expected to uphold certain standards, right?"

That was true, way too true. "Right. And I didn't uphold those standards. My sister said it. As ugly as it sounds, I had a one-night stand. With you."

"You're not a one-night-stand woman. We both know that. And so does this town. And all I'm asking you to consider is, what if it wasn't a one-night stand?"

"But it *was*." She rested back in the chair again. "Oh, Ross. This is silly. Silly and sad. As well as unnecessary. I have to tell you, as far as I'm concerned, the worst is over. The town of Whitehorn is not going to be nearly as hard on me as my own family has been."

"You're sure about that?"

"I'm as sure as I need to be."

He gave her another of those long, probing looks. Then he grunted. "You know, you may be right. Everybody in this town seems to adore you. You're almost as popular as little Jenny McCallum. It's probably not you they'll be blaming for what we did last night."

"You're saying they're going to blame you?" That thought hadn't even occurred to her.

He was nodding—and that rueful smile was tipping up the corners of his beautiful mouth. "After all, I'm the outsider. The lawyer. Since Wendell Hargrove got himself shipped off to the slammer, lawyers seem to have a bad name around here."

"Maybe they won't blame anyone. Maybe they'll just gossip for a while, and then get over it."

The rueful smile was still there. "Maybe you're right."

She stood.

Ross got the message. "So. No fake engagement, then?"

"I'm afraid not."

"Bad idea, huh?"

She let a shrug answer that one.

And Ross knew it was time to go. She looked beat. Shadows of fatigue marred the tender skin beneath those wide blue eyes. He shouldn't have come in the first place. He should have called her concerning the missing shoe and let it be at that.

"Sorry," he heard himself say. Then he swore. "I seem to keep saying that—as if it might help."

"It's all right."

"Listen, if there's anything—"

"There's not. Honestly."

"Well, then…" He cast about for something else to say. He was stalling, plain and simple. It was time to go.

But he didn't want to go.

She fixed that. "I'll walk you to the door."

Damn. He wanted…more. Wanted things he had no right to want. More nights like last night. More time in her company, to listen to her laugh, to watch her smile. To pretend...

Yes, all right. To pretend. That he was a different kind of man than he really was. That the world was a better place than he'd ever found it to be. That someday, more than an empty, expensive house would be waiting when he got home.

Well, he wasn't going to be allowed to pretend. He might as well quit stalling and get used to the idea. "It's all right. I can find my way out." He started walking.

She fell in behind him as he went past. He had known that she would. He had taken her innocence and apparently created all kinds of havoc between her and her family. But she was still the kind of woman who wouldn't make a man find the exit on his own.

In the small foyer she slid around him and opened the door. "Goodbye, Ross."

It sounded final. Way too damn final.

He looked at her mouth, thought, *One more kiss. That's all I want. Just one final kiss.*

He must have possessed some last flimsy shred of integrity, because he didn't reach for her.

He said, "Goodbye, Lynn," and he walked out the door.

Lynn shut it behind him. And then she just stood there, staring toward the stairs, but not really seeing them, wishing he had gone ahead and kissed her as she'd known he wanted to.

Oh, she couldn't help it. Her heart went out to him. He'd looked so grim. So determined. Determined to save her reputation with a lie.

A lie.

What had Winona chanted that morning?

A ring and a lie, that was it. A lie that would bring truth.

Could Ross's suggestion that they fake an engagement be that lie?

No, that was foolish thinking. Hopeful, mad, crazy thinking.

Only a lawyer would have come up with an insane scheme like that.

And only a hopeless romantic would consider going along with it because of something Winona Cobbs had chanted during an impromptu early-morning trance out on Route 17.

Only a hopeless romantic who had gone and let herself fall in love in the space of one night.

Lynn drooped back against the door she had closed on Ross Garrison.

Was that it? She brought up both hands and rubbed her tired, grainy eyes. Was she in love with Ross Garrison?

Oh, Lord, it did feel like it. It truly did.

And, hopeless romantic that she was, she just couldn't stop herself from wishing for more. Wishing for the impossible.

That Ross Garrison might have fallen in love, too.

Lynn dropped her hands to her sides and looked down at her aching feet.

No.

He was a sophisticated man. He wasn't going to decide he was in love just because he'd spent the night with her. He was wary of loving. She could see it in his eyes, that coldness—a coldness that seemed to mask a deep hurt.

She let out a small, tortured laugh and cast her

gaze toward the old-fashioned tulip-shaded chandelier overhead.

Only a hopeless romantic, she thought again. Only a hopeless romantic would find suffering hidden in a pair of cold eyes.

But then again, if they were to pretend to be sweethearts, they would have to spend time together, wouldn't they? And, over time, maybe she could break down the wall he'd put around his heart—maybe, deep down, he was hoping she would do just that.

Now, *that* was a crazy idea.

To let herself even imagine that—

But wait just a darn minute.

Why shouldn't she imagine?

Why shouldn't she dream?

Why shouldn't she just be what she was, a hopeless romantic, willing to take a psychic's advice?

To teach her prince—and to believe in the magic of love.

Energy seemed to flow back into her body. She straightened, turned—and yanked open the door.

He hadn't left. The Mercedes was still there, a dark, imposing shadow at the curb.

That was a good sign, wasn't it? That he was still sitting there in that fancy SUV of his, that he hadn't yet managed to turn the key in the ignition and drive away?

She could see him in there. He had turned his head. He was watching her.

Wrapping her arms around herself to ward off the chill in the night air, she walked out the door and down the front steps.

The window on the passenger side slid down. Ross leaned across the console toward her.

She said, "Would you come back inside, please?" And then she turned and marched right back to the house without giving him a chance to say a word in reply.

She led him to the living room again, gestured at the sofa as she had before. This time he sat down. And then immediately demanded, "What is it?"

"I've been thinking."

"About what?"

"I have a few questions."

Those cold eyes narrowed marginally. "Questions about what?"

"Well, say that we did what you suggested...."

He shifted impatiently. "We're not going to do it, so what does it matter?"

"Bear with me. What if we did what you suggested, pretended that we really were engaged? Then what? How would it end? Did you think about that?"

"Lynn. I don't see what—"

"Just humor me. Did you think about that?"

"Yes," he confessed. "I did."

"And?"

"I thought that you'd break up with me. In a few weeks, or a month. You'd decide I wasn't the right man for you, after all—which is only the truth. I'm not the right man for you." His eyes had darkened, making her wonder what secrets they hid from her.

She dared to inquire, "So you're telling me I shouldn't get my hopes up, is that it? There's no chance you might decide you really do want to marry me, after all?"

"Lynn." His voice was tender. And suddenly, so

were his eyes. "You wouldn't want to find yourself married to someone like me."

"Oh, and why is that?" she asked, much more casually than she felt.

For a moment she thought he might actually tell her. But then he only repeated what he'd said before. "You just wouldn't, that's all."

She longed to ask why again. And again and again. Until he told her the secrets of his shadowed heart. But no. Not now. There would be time for that in the weeks ahead.

She spoke briskly. "Well, all right, then. It will last for a month. And I'll be the one who breaks it off when the month is up."

"What are you saying?"

"I'm saying that I'm taking you up on your offer. We'll pretend you're my fiancé. For one month."

There was blank disbelief on his face. "You're kidding."

"No. I'm as serious as a visit to the principal's office."

"But I thought you…" The words trailed off into nothing. He seemed totally at a loss as to what to say next.

That was all right with her. She knew exactly what *she* wanted to say. "There would have to be certain ground rules."

He actually gulped. "Ground rules?"

"We would have to really spend time together. See each other two or three times a week, at least. I mean, that's what people who are going to get married usually do, isn't it?"

"Well. Yes. Yes, I suppose they do. But—"

She cut him off before he could get rolling with

any more objections. "Could you handle that? Seeing me two or three times a week for the next month or so?"

He scowled. "Of course I could."

"You don't look terribly thrilled at the prospect."

He swore. "Of course I'm thrilled."

She chose not to belabor that point, but went on. "And you wouldn't be able to have any other lady friends—I mean, until the month is up and it's time for me to decide that you're not the man for me."

He looked insulted. "I don't have any 'lady friends' currently—other than you."

She felt a blush rising and resisted the urge to draw attention to it by pressing cool hands to her hot cheeks. "Well. I suppose after last night, I would count as a lady friend."

He said nothing. But what she saw in his eyes made a thousand little fluttery things come to life in her solar plexus. She tightened her stomach muscles, hoping to make them be still. They wouldn't, so she set her sights on ignoring them.

"All right, then," she said. "We'll see each other often. It will be exclusive while it lasts. And I think…" She cast about for a delicate way of putting what she had to say next.

"You think *what?*"

"I think we'd better avoid nights like last night."

He got the message. "No sex, you mean."

"Yes. That's what I mean."

"That's fine." He sounded more grim than sincere. "It's appropriate, I think."

"Yes. I think so, too." And she did. Or at least, the Lynn Taylor she'd always thought she was until last night did.

But that other Lynn Taylor—the one who had worn a red cashmere dress and slept in his arms—*that* Lynn Taylor felt her throat clutching with regret.

He was leaning forward in the chair now. "Are you sure you want to do this?"

"Yes."

He shook his head. But he said, "Okay. It's settled." He rose to his feet.

She followed him to the door for the second time that night. Before he went out, she told him, "We might as well get started tomorrow."

He looked at her sideways. "Get started?"

She nodded. "Since it's Saturday, I won't be at the school. You can pick me up here. At noon?"

"To do what?"

"We'll have lunch together. At the Hip Hop Café."

Chapter Ten

He arrived right on time. He was wearing a different jacket again, different slacks and *another* pair of beautiful calfskin boots. He was also smiling.

Irritation sizzled through her. Here they were about to stroll into the Hip Hop together, as bold as you please, to pretend to be sweethearts—and he was smiling as if the idea actually pleased him. She'd had second thoughts for hours after he left last night— was *still* having second thoughts, as a matter of fact.

And beyond her second thoughts, she'd had a terrible time deciding what to wear. Everything she owned, except the red dress, which would hardly be suitable for a casual Saturday lunch at the local café, was just…boring. Brown and gray. Variations on the same monotonous theme.

For something like this, she needed *color,* for heaven's sake. In fact, as soon as she got the opportunity, she was heading for Billings to take care of the problem.

She'd settled on a pair of black jeans and a fluffy white sweater. Both hugged her new curves, and the sweater had a rather flattering V neck. It was the best she could do on such short notice.

His dark glance flicked over her. The appreciation in it eased her nerves just a little. ''Ready?''

''You seem awfully cheerful about this, all of a sudden.'' The edginess she felt was there in her tone.

He either didn't notice—or decided not to let it bother him. ''Hey, we agreed to do this. No need to act like we're headed for a funeral.''

She opened her mouth to let out a sharp retort— and had to admit to herself that he probably had a point. ''Here.'' She held out a white legal-sized envelope.

''What's that? A subpoena?''

''Very funny. It's the report on Jenny you asked me for.'' She'd been awake half the night anyway, so she'd decided she might as well make use of the time.

''Great.'' He tucked it into an inside pocket of his jacket. ''Shall we go?''

Let's not, she thought, a shiver of dread slithering up her spine at the prospect of walking into the Hip Hop on this man's arm. After all, by now a lot of people in town had to know how and where she'd spent her birthday night. The fact that they were ''engaged'' would help—but as the old saying went, they were only shutting the barn door after the cow had got out.

''Looks like we've got a major case of cold feet

going here," he said, still in that annoyingly light-hearted tone.

"Not at all," she baldly lied. "Just let me get my coat."

The Hip Hop Café was decorated in what Lynn had always thought of as Early Thrift Store. The tables were covered in red-checked oilcloths and none of the chairs matched. A stunning variety of bargain-basement treasures adorned the walls, everything from framed samplers with little homilies embroidered on them to a velvet painting of Geronimo, and a huge moth-eaten moose head.

A definite hush descended when Lynn walked in on Ross's arm. Lynn spotted Lily Mae Wheeler immediately. The bighearted busybody sat at her favorite table, near the far wall, where she would have a good view of whoever came in and out. Winona Cobbs sat beside her.

At the sight of the two women, Lynn held Ross's arm tighter. He responded by laying his big, warm hand over hers and granting her a smile that could only be defined as fond and reassuring.

Real or part of the act? she started to wonder—and then told herself it didn't matter. He might be a little too cheerful to suit her at the moment, but he was here, at her side, facing her town with her. *That* was what mattered.

Lily Mae banished the silence with a girlish giggle. "If it isn't our lovebirds!"

Ross pulled Lynn a fraction closer. She wanted to sag against him—and jerk away at the same time. She did neither, just plastered a smile on her face and hoped she didn't look as frazzled as she felt.

And then he actually nuzzled her hair, right there at the door to the Hip Hop, with everyone watching. "Remember," he whispered, under the pretense of nuzzling. "Coming here was your idea...."

Lynn decided not to reply. She didn't have time, anyway. Lily Mae had started waving. The bracelet on her arm, which appeared to be made of heavy gold links and big hunks of caramel-colored rock, rattled imperiously. "Come on now, you two. Mosey on over here and say hi."

They moseyed, murmuring hellos to people they knew as they moved by the other tables. To Lynn, the short walk felt like a marathon.

At last they stood at Lily Mae's table. The good-natured gossip wasted no time. She got straight to the point. "I hear a wedding's in the offing."

Lynn slid a glance toward Winona. The older woman was smiling. It seemed an alert kind of smile. Lynn sincerely hoped she wouldn't choose this opportunity to slip into another trance and start babbling away about princes and rings and dark nights of fear and misery.

"Well, hon?" demanded Lily. "Are you and this fella getting hitched or not?"

Lynn cleared her throat. "Uh, we..."

Ross picked up the ball. "Yes, Mrs. Wheeler. Lynn has made me the happiest man alive. She's agreed to become Mrs. Ross Garrison."

Lynn shot him a quelling glance, thinking, the happiest man alive? Laying it on a bit thick, aren't you?

He gave her that too-ardent smile of his in response.

"Congratulations," said Lily Mae. "You are a very lucky man."

"I know." He sounded utterly sincere.

So why did she want to brain him?

"I don't see a ring." Lily Mae clucked her tongue. "Lynn, honey, where is it?"

"Yes," said Winona sweetly. "There must be a ring."

Lynn shifted her glance to the psychic again. The woman still looked fully conscious, thank God—though wasn't there something just a little bit sly in those wise eyes of hers? "I, uh, well...this has all been so sudden. We haven't..."

Ross came to her rescue again. "We're on our way to take care of that. As soon as we've eaten."

"Uh. We are?" The incredulous words escaped her before she had a chance to consider how strange they would sound.

Lily Mae granted Ross a raised eyebrow.

Ross didn't miss a beat. "It was a surprise. But I guess the cat's out of the bag now. The minute we leave here, I'm taking her to a certain jewelry store I know of in Billings so that she can choose the one she wants."

"Well, now." Lily Mae was beaming. "Isn't that just lovely?"

"Yes," agreed Winona. "Lovely."

"Do get her a nice big diamond, Mr. Garrison," Lily Mae instructed. "There's nothing like a diamond to make a girl feel a man's devotion."

"I'll remember that," Ross said. "And now, if you ladies will excuse us?"

The big brown rocks on Lily Mae's bracelet

started rattling again. "Go on, go on. Find yourselves a nice private corner."

Lynn waited until Janie, the waitress who managed the place, had seated them and taken their order before she leaned toward Ross and whispered, "Billings? We're going to Billings?"

He shrugged. "I had to say something when Lily Mae asked. And you do need a ring. Darling."

She didn't like the way he said that. Darling. As if it were their own private joke.

Or maybe she did like it. And only wished it had sounded a tad more sincere.

There was a small plastic stand in the center of the table, with pictures of various desserts on it. Ross picked it up. "Hmm. Banana cream pie. Looks good."

"We haven't even had our sandwiches yet."

"I'm just planning ahead."

"Well," she said sourly, "don't plan for me. I'm skipping dessert."

He set the stand down. "Maybe I can tempt you."

She thought of chocolate truffle cake. Of vanilla bean ice cream, melting on her tongue.

And she knew that *he* knew what she was thinking.

"Not today," she said firmly.

He heaved a big fake sigh and set the dessert stand back in its place. "There's nothing wrong with a little dessert now and then."

"No, there is not. But I…have to watch my weight."

"Your weight, huh?" It was a taunt, pure and simple. He didn't believe her. He thought that this exchange was about the way he had tempted her two nights before.

And it was. Mostly.

"I do have to watch my weight," she said, feeling defensive. And irritated. And foolish, as well.

"Why? Your weight is just right."

That pleased her. It truly did. Too bad she didn't feel in a mood to be pleased. "It didn't used to be—and do you think we could talk about something else?" She cast a significant glance around the bustling restaurant. No one seemed to be listening, but you could never tell.

"Sure." He rested his forearms on the table, leaned toward her and whispered, "And what would you like to talk about?"

She whispered right back. "Just…keep it light, okay? Act affectionate."

"I can do that."

"I noticed." You're very good at deception, she was thinking. Too good…

Janie wove her way through the lunchtime crowd, bearing their sandwiches. With a high degree of relief Lynn watched the waitress approach. "Let's just eat and get out of here."

"Your wish is my command."

Twenty minutes later they were in his Mercedes, on their way to Billings.

"It's a beautiful day," he said as they sped up the highway, barbed wire and drift fences flowing past on either side. "The sun is shining. The cattle are grazing. The sky is as blue as your eyes." He sent her a quick look, then focused on the road again and asked flatly, "What's the matter now?"

Oh, nothing much, she thought. Except I think I love you. And I wish this was for real.

He shot her another look. "Have you changed your mind about this thing, is that it?"

"No." She really hadn't. She wanted this chance with him, wanted to turn this lie into truth.

"Then why are you behaving like a damn brat? This isn't like you."

She longed to turn on him, to screech, How do you know what I'm like? You've only known me for two days!

But she stopped herself.

He was right. She *was* behaving like a brat. She was *feeling* like a brat. Testy and ready to pitch herself a hissy fit.

And it *wasn't* like her. She did have faults, a number of them. But sheer brattiness wasn't one.

She just...didn't like this deception. She didn't approve of it. Any more than she approved of the fact that she'd gone to bed with this man on the first night she'd met him.

But she had done it. *Was* doing it, acting out a lie.

And if she intended to keep on doing it, she'd better make her peace with it somehow, now, hadn't she?

He asked, sounding honestly concerned, "Are you worried about your family?"

Her heart contracted. "Yes," she admitted in a small voice.

"It was really that bad? The scene with them yesterday?"

He was offering her a chance to talk about it, as much as saying he was willing to listen. A warmth spread through her. It wasn't exactly what she'd planned; she wanted to get *him* to open up to *her*.

But maybe if she shared a few hard truths of her own, he'd feel safer sharing his.

She confessed, "It was awful. My stepmother called me a snake in the grass. And Arlene said I was trash. And Trish...well, you can imagine."

Apparently he could. "Trish sobbed and shouted and accused you of stealing her boyfriend—me."

All Lynn could manage right then was a small sound in the affirmative.

"I was not her boyfriend, Lynn. Not by any stretch of the imagination. I made that very clear to her. Repeatedly." He shifted his grip on the steering wheel. "I suppose she told you that she quit."

"Yes, she did." She looked over at him. His eyes remained on the road ahead. "I guess you're relieved—and never mind. Don't answer that. I understand. I do know my sister...." She heaved a sigh. "She moved out of my house. She said she wasn't going to spend another minute around someone like me."

"I have to say it. It sounds to me like you're better off without her. And Jewel and Arlene, too."

Lynn looked away from him, out her side window at a patch of rocky outcroppings and dry scrub brush. "I've thought that once or twice myself."

"You're mumbling."

She turned to him. "They are difficult. And I guess they've kept me down, over the years. I wanted them to love me. And maybe I hid my true self from them, to make our lives run more smoothly. I'm not willing to do that anymore. And so there's a problem. But I still remember Jewel fussing over me, staying up all night to watch over me when I was fourteen and had pneumonia. I remember her hand on my forehead, checking my fever. There *was* love in that hand.

"And once, a boy at school called me a big, fat cow. Trish spit in his face and then blacked his eye. Said he'd better not disrespect her sister if he knew what was good for him. She got suspended for a week for doing that."

The smallest hint of a smile lifted the corners of his mouth. "Trish is a fighter. I'll say that much for her."

"Yes. And Arlene..."

"Arlene what?"

"Well, six years ago, when she married Clyde—that's her husband, Clyde—she really wanted me for a bridesmaid, made a big deal about my dress. She wanted me to have a color I liked, wanted the fit to flatter my...generous curves. And then, when she threw her bouquet, she threw it to me." Lynn couldn't help chuckling. "I don't think Trish has ever forgiven her. But I guess Arlene figured I needed that bouquet more than Trish did."

Ross looked at her then. "Arlene miscalculated."

"I'll take that as a compliment."

"Good. I meant it as one."

They shared a smile before he turned back to the road.

She said, "So if you ask me, do I care if Jewel and my stepsisters ever speak to me again? Well, in spite of everything, the answer would have to be yes. Yes, I do care. They are my family. And I honestly do not want to lose them. And somehow, I'm going to find a way to mend this awful rift between us."

They rode in silence for a time. Then she asked, "What about *your* family?"

"What about them?" The words sounded casual, but his real meaning came through loud and clear: keep away.

"You said you're not close...."

"We're not."

She tried one more time. "You said your parents are dead. What did they die of?"

He took so long to answer, she began to wonder if he'd heard the question.

But at last he said, "It's not something I talk about, as a rule. People like their lawyers to come from solid, dependable backgrounds. Since I don't, I generally try to gloss over the subject whenever anyone brings it up. I don't lie about it. I just...avoid getting into it."

"You're asking me not to repeat what you're going to tell me?"

"That's right."

She felt slightly breathless. This was progress, wasn't it? One of the secrets she saw in his eyes, revealed? "All right. You have my word. I won't say anything to anyone."

After a minute, he said, "My father had a few problems. He liked to gamble. He liked to drink. And he liked to fool around with other men's wives. My mother just liked to drink. She died of liver failure. And *he* died when he got caught in another man's bed. The other man showed up unexpectedly. With a shotgun. Not a pretty way to go."

Expressions of sympathy rose to her lips. She did not utter them. Instead, she reached across the distance between them and squeezed his arm.

He kept looking straight ahead. "Hardly a princely beginning."

She told him softly, "You've come a long way."

"As I think I mentioned the other night, I knew what I wanted."

"And you went after it."

He flashed her a look. His eyes were black agates, smooth and impenetrable. "That's right. Nothing stood in my way."

She took her hand off his arm and retreated to her own seat, wanting to probe further...but not quite daring to.

Later, she thought. Over time. It's one thing we do have because of this lie.

Time...

He bought her an absurdly expensive engagement and wedding ring set, with diamonds all along the wedding band and an engagement stone the size of a brand-new eraser at the tip of a number-two pencil. Hard and bright as his eyes, the thing glittered on her hand.

She tried to argue that there was no need, that they could just as well buy a manufactured stone. The false stones were beautiful; they looked like the real thing. And a fake stone was more than good enough, considering the circumstances.

But he said, "We don't want to let Lily Mae down, do we? And anyway, why the hell shouldn't we get the real thing? I can afford it. And I like the way it looks on your hand."

"Ross. We don't *need* it. And we certainly don't have to bother with a wedding band."

"Yes, we do, if we want this engagement ring. The two are a matched set." He turned to the salesman, who was standing far enough away to give them a bit of privacy, watching them with a slightly baffled look on his face. "We'll take them. She'll wear the engagement ring."

The salesman, all smiles now, trotted off down the row of glass cases to write up the big sale.

When they left the jewelry store, Ross wanted to take her to dinner.

She made a face at him. "You really do want to see what I look like carrying an extra twenty or thirty pounds around, don't you?"

He admitted that it was a little early yet to eat. "So what shall we do until then?"

She glanced down at the ring on her hand. It caught the sunlight and gleamed at her. She felt…just wonderful.

It might all be a lie, but what a beautiful lie. Ross's ring on her hand. Ahead of her, an evening with him.

A number of evenings. At least a month's worth.

"We could go to ZooMontana. But I think it closes at five."

He glanced at his watch. "That's only an hour away. Better think of something else."

She suggested an art center. He said that would be fine with him.

So for the next two hours they wandered the rooms of a newly expanded museum, admiring the work of top Western artists—and holding hands, though there really wasn't any need to. They didn't see anyone they knew.

And then, later, since he insisted, they went out to eat at a restaurant in a nearby hotel. There, though he tried his best to tempt her, she refused dessert.

It was after ten when they got back to her house.

She wanted to invite him in, but decided that might be taking temptation a little too far.

He kissed her on her front step. "Just in case the neighbors are watching," he whispered as his mouth covered hers.

She gave herself up to that kiss, sliding her arms over his chest, grasping his wide shoulders and sighing as his tongue touched hers.

By the time he pulled away, she felt just dazed and dreamy enough to reconsider the idea of asking him inside. Really, what harm could it do? It *was* Saturday night. She didn't have to work tomorrow.

He must have known what she was thinking. He whispered, "Better not. It wouldn't be wise."

Reluctantly she stepped back. They murmured "Good night" in unison and she stood on the step, watching as he strode over the yellowing grass of her small front lawn to the Mercedes. After he got in, he turned and looked at her from the driver's seat before he started up the big SUV.

She waved. He waved back. Just like a smitten lover. As if he couldn't bear to lose sight of her, though he knew it was time to go.

Inside the house, she hung her coat in the closet. Then, feeling light as the bubbles in a glass of champagne, she ran up the stairs.

She was giggling to herself when she passed Trish's room. The door was ajar. Lynn peeked in.

Sometime during the day Trish must have come for her furniture. All that remained were a few dog-eared women's magazines scattered across the scuffed hardwood floor and a number of fat, gray dust bunnies. They fled away beneath Lynn's feet as she entered the echoing space.

"Oh, Trish..." Lynn sighed at the bare walls and the uncurtained windows. "What did you do, store it all?" There certainly wouldn't be room for it at Arlene and Clyde's, where Trish would have to share a room with their three-year-old, Darla Sue.

Lynn bent and picked up the magazines. A little time, she thought. A week or so. And I'll call Arlene's.

Her stomach tightened painfully at the thought. Rejection. That was what she would get for her effort. At least at first. But it had to be done.

She spoke aloud to the emptiness again. "First, though, I think I'll give it a little time."

Yes. A little time...

Chapter Eleven

The next afternoon, Danielle appeared at Lynn's door. She'd dropped Sara off at the McCallums before she came.

"To give us a few minutes alone," she said. "I love my child. But the phrase 'monopolize the conversation' must have been invented with Sara in mind."

Lynn led her friend to the breakfast nook, where she offered a chair and a hot cup of coffee.

"Rumor has it you're engaged," Danielle said. "And that diamond on your finger leads me to believe that rumor has it right." Danielle set her mug down. "Let me see."

Lynn held her hand across the table, regret squeezing her heart. She wanted to tell her friend the truth.

But no. This was her lie. Hers and Ross's. Danielle didn't need to know, didn't need to carry the extra burden of having to lie along with them, because that was what Lynn would have to ask her to do.

"It's absolutely gorgeous." Danielle let go of Lynn's hand and looked up. "Happy?"

"Ecstatic."

"Boy, when I give a makeover, things happen, don't they?"

"You're the best fairy godmother this Cinderella ever had."

Danielle fiddled with her mug a little, pushing it along the table from right to left. Then she asked, gingerly, "Jewel and your sisters?"

Lynn simply shook her head.

"What is the matter with them?" Danielle muttered. It was a rhetorical question.

But Lynn did have an answer for it. "Well, Trish had a…what should I call it? A crush. A big one. On Ross. She thinks I betrayed her." Lynn paused. She was giving her friend a chance to ask *Well, did you?* though she had no idea how she would reply. But Danielle didn't ask. So Lynn continued, "Trish quit her job with Ross and moved over to Arlene's."

"Grim."

"That's the word."

"I hate to say it, but—"

"I know, I know. I'm better off without them."

"Sorry. Good friends and hairdressers, they tell you the truth."

"You may be right. But I love them. And I'm going to work things out with them, I really am."

"Good luck. You'll need it."

"I wish I could say you were wrong about that."

On Tuesday and Thursday of the following week, Ross appeared at the door to Lynn's classroom right after she'd sent her young charges home for the day. He took her to lunch. At the Hip Hop on Tuesday and the State Street Grill on Thursday.

On Thursday he told her he'd hired a new secretary, Mrs. Beatrice Simms. Lynn had never met her. Mrs. Simms, it turned out, was relatively new to Whitehorn.

"I can tell by your expression," Lynn said. "Mrs. Simms is a keeper."

"She seems…very organized. And efficient."

Lynn knew he was trying to be tactful, for the sake of her loyalty to Trish. "I really do hope she works out," she said, meaning it. "And now all you need is a new housekeeper, right?"

He grunted. "Do I ever. The dust on my tables is so thick, I can write myself memos in it. The woman came on Tuesday. You'd never guess it, though— except that she left a load of wet sheets in the dryer."

"Did she, um, happen to find my shoe?"

Something flashed in his eyes; there and then gone. A fleeting memory, she felt certain, of the night they had shared. "If she did, she didn't bother to inform me."

The red shoes had been expensive. And like the cashmere dress, they were mementos of that magical, forbidden night. Even if she never wore them again, Lynn wanted to keep them. "Do you think she might have thrown it away?"

"Anything's possible, knowing that woman. I'll talk to her next Tuesday, all right? And I'll look around again."

"It's really strange, don't you think? That it would just…disappear like that?"

He shrugged. "It has to be there somewhere."

She wondered for a moment if maybe he had found it himself, after all. If, for some reason, he hesitated to give it back to her. Maybe he wanted a memento of his own. She felt her cheeks grow warm at the thought.

He was frowning. "Lynn. I swear to you. I wouldn't keep your red shoe."

She hastened to put his mind at ease. "No, of course you wouldn't. But if you do find it—"

"You'll get it. I promise. Are you ready for dessert?"

She sweetly told him no.

On Friday night he escorted her to the Halloween dance at the Grange hall. She borrowed a cat costume from one of her fellow teachers for the event. Ross came as a riverboat gambler, complete with embroidered vest, string tie and fake moustache.

Trish was there, dressed in red satin, with black lace petticoats showing underneath: a dance-hall queen. She locked eyes with Lynn once. Lynn watched the emotions chase themselves across her sister's dainty, heart-shaped face: surprise first, then honest affection, then hurt—and finally anger. The flashing series of expressions lasted mere seconds. Then Trish whipped her head away and flounced off. Lynn looped her dangling cat tail over her arm and asked Ross to dance with her.

"Best offer I've had all evening," he said.

She focused on the singularly sweet sensation of having his arms around her and tried to block out the nagging awareness that she needed to do something to make contact with her family again.

When Ross took her home at one in the morning, he kissed her on her front step, just as he had kissed her the night they bought the ring—and both of the days he had taken her to lunch.

But he didn't come in.

She didn't ask him and he didn't suggest it. They were both exercising caution, avoiding any situation where they might be alone in the proximity of a bed.

That Monday evening, Lynn forced herself to pick up the phone and punch up Arlene's number. Jewel answered. Lynn had barely said hello when she heard the click and the dial tone. She set the phone back in its cradle and tried not to let herself get too depressed about the fact that her stepmother had hung up on her.

The next day after school, Lynn drove to Billings to cheer herself up. She wandered through the stores at the Rimrock Mall and bought three skirts, five bright-colored sweaters, three pair of shoes that actually had heels on them and two cashmere blend jackets, one traffic-light red and one a sort of misty mauve color. She also bought a new coat of bright red wool.

It was after nine at night when she got home. She was putting her new clothes away when the doorbell rang.

It was Ross. "I called three times since five. No answer."

Pleasure washed through her, at the sight of him, at the thought that he'd wanted to talk to her so much, he'd been calling practically on the hour throughout the evening.

"You could at least get a damn answering machine. That way, I could leave you messages, so you'd know how irritated I was that you weren't there.''

''I had an answering machine. Or rather, Trish did. She took it with her when she left.''

''I'll buy you one.''

''I'll take care of it myself, I promise—and do you want to come in?''

He smiled then, causing her spirits to soar and her pulse to start racing.

''Well, come on,'' she said, not letting herself think that they were breaking their own silent agreement to avoid being truly alone together. She pulled him over the threshold and led him to the kitchen. ''Want something to drink? Nonalcoholic, I'm afraid.''

He accepted a glass of apple juice and sat down. ''So, where have you been since five o'clock?''

''Shopping. In Billings.''

''Shopping for what?''

''Clothing that is not brown.''

''Did you find anything?''

''I certainly did. If my credit card could groan, you'd hear sounds of misery coming from my purse.'' She brushed by him on her way to a chair.

He caught her hand. A warm shiver traveled up her arm and spread out from there, up to her cheeks, down into her solar plexus...

''What?'' she asked, as if she didn't know.

Instead of answering, he stood and pulled her close.

She braced her hands on his chest. Her heart was knocking away, too hard and way too fast. ''Ross...''

''Shh.''

And he kissed her, sliding his hand down to press the center of her back, bringing her up tight against him, so that she had no doubt how truly glad he was to see her.

She easily could have stood there, kissing him, feeling her body heating and readying, right on into the next millennium. But of course, if she'd done that, they wouldn't be standing for long. They'd end up prone. On her bed…

She pushed at his chest, murmuring his name again, in warning—and regret.

"Sorry." He let her go and stepped back.

She tried to make light of it. "See? It's just not safe for us to be alone together."

He didn't take well to her teasing, not at that particular moment. "What does that mean? You want me to go?"

"No, of course not. Sit down. Drink your juice."

"'Drink your juice,'" he parroted coldly. "You sound just like a kindergarten teacher."

"I *am* a kindergarten teacher."

"Well, I'm no kindergartner."

"Ross. Please don't be angry."

He was scowling at her now. "I shouldn't have come here." He swore. "I don't know why the hell I did."

She wanted to touch him, but she feared it would only make things worse. "Maybe you just…wanted to see me. There's nothing wrong with that."

"Isn't there?"

She refused to let him goad her. "No. There's not. I'm glad you're here."

"Are you?"

"Yes, I am. Now, sit down. And we'll talk."

"About what?"

"Whatever you'd like to talk about." She listed a few safe subjects. "The weather. My problem students. The exemplary Mrs. Simms." And thought of a few that probably weren't so safe: your childhood. Your ex-wife...

He was watching her mouth. "I've got other things than talking on my mind."

She spoke tenderly. "Yes, I know. But don't think about that."

"Easy for you to say."

"No. No, it's not, actually."

That seemed to mollify him. Enough that he dropped into his chair again.

She sat down herself. "Now I'm going to ask you how your day went. And you're going to tell me. And when you're done telling me, I'll tell *you* all about *my* day. And after that, if we're both still awake, we'll think of something else to talk about."

He looked slightly bewildered—and so handsome her heart ached. "This is crazy, isn't it?"

"Which? Pretending we're engaged or your coming here tonight?"

"Both."

"We could stop." Oh, why had she said that? What if he said that he thought they *should* stop?

But he didn't. He stood again. "It's too soon for you to call it off. We need to give it a few more weeks."

Do we? a part of her wanted to ask. Do we really?

But that would only bring them a little closer to an ending.

She didn't want it to end. Not ever.

But if it *was* going to end, she'd take every minute she could get until then.

"I'm going," he said. "It's after ten. And we both have to work tomorrow."

"I'm still glad you came."

"Crazy," he said again, musingly this time.

She got up and followed him to the door.

On Thursday Lynn called Arlene's house again. Arlene herself answered this time. And she didn't hang up—at least, not immediately.

"Oh." Arlene made a humphing sound. "It's you. Are you all right?"

"I'm fine, Arlene."

A silence, then, "I suppose I should tell you that I feel kind of bad that I called you trash. I don't really think you're trash."

"I know."

"But what you did was rotten and low."

"I'm sorry you think that."

Arlene humphed again. And then the line went dead.

Lynn decided to call that conversation progress. She stopped in at the drugstore the next day and bought three all-occasion greeting cards, each one with "I love you and miss you" sentiments inside. She mailed them off right away—one each for Jewel and Arlene and Trish.

That weekend, on Saturday, she and Ross drove to Billings again. They had dinner and saw a movie. During the drive back, Lynn tried to get him to talk more about his family, about his life before he'd come to Whitehorn. He grudgingly admitted that he had worked as a ranch hand for two summers while he was in his teens. The ranch had been a huge one, bigger than the Kincaid spread, not far from Billings. The rancher had taken a liking to him and ended up helping him, getting letters of recommendation for him when he'd started applying for college scholarships. The rancher had even had a few friends who were Princeton alumni.

"He pulled some strings, I guess you could say. And that's how I ended up getting a scholarship to go there."

Lynn jumped in with both feet then. "Where did your wife go to college?"

He looked straight ahead. "I'm not married."

"But…you *were* married? When you lived in Denver?"

"Yes."

"What was her name?"

"Elana."

"What was she like?"

He did cast her a glance then, an unreadable one. "My marriage didn't work out. My wife died. And I'd rather not talk about it."

Lynn did a double take. "She *died?* But I heard you were divorced."

A low, disgusted sound escaped him. "From Trish, right?"

"Well, yes, but—"

"Look. I might have told your sister I was divorced. If my wife hadn't died, I would have been. The marriage was over at that point, I promise you."

"But—"

He cut her off again. "In my experience, if a man says he's divorced, people hesitate to pry. On the other hand, if he says he's a widower, he's fair game—for expressions of sympathy. And questions. A lot of questions. From 'How long were you married?' to 'How did she die?' I didn't want to get into all that, so yes, it's possible I said I was divorced.''

"But you're not. You're a widower."

"Yes. I'm a widower. Now let's talk about something else."

"I'd just like to know—"

"It's the past. It's done with."

Lynn didn't believe that. Not for a minute. "Is it?"

"Drop it, Lynn. I mean it." The words were hard as granite rocks.

Lynn subsided into silence. Not a word was spoken through the remainder of the drive home.

When they got to her house, he walked her to her door. But he didn't kiss her. And he didn't call the next day.

On Monday Lynn learned that Mrs. Parchly, the school secretary, planned to hire an assistant, someone who would be part-time clerical and part-time teacher's aide. The pay was modest to start, but the benefit package would be a good one. It occurred to Lynn that Trish had the basic qualifications for the job.

She stewed about whether or not to try to approach Trish on the subject. So far, Trish had hardly proved a model employee. It might not even be fair to the school for Lynn to recommend her. If Trish were hired and made a mess of it, Lynn would feel at least partly to blame.

She was still trying to decide what to do when she got home at four—and found Trish sitting on her front step.

"Can I…come in? Just for a few minutes?"

"Sure."

They went to the breakfast nook and sat across from each other at the round maple table.

"Thanks for the card," Trish said in a tiny, lost-sounding voice.

"You're welcome."

"When I got it, I just sat down and cried."

"I didn't mean for you to cry."

"Well, I did. I cried. And I thought about you and how you're my sister and…well, men can come and go—but a person only gets so many sisters in her life." Trish folded her hands on the table and then stared at them, her soft lower lip quivering. "I guess…I've got to admit it…." Trish faltered. Lynn held her breath.

She let it out when Trish made herself go on. "You didn't really steal Ross Garrison from me. He never even liked me much, anyway. I guess I'm just not his type. But I…I thought I could *make* him like me. And then, when it turned out he wanted you, well, I was so jealous, I could have kicked a hog barefooted. You know how I get when things don't go my way…."

Lynn did know. She also knew how much grit and love it had taken for spoiled little Trish to come here today. She reached out, then thought better of it. She folded her own hands, just to have something to do with them.

Trish spotted the ring. "Wow. That's some diamond."

Lynn met her sister's eyes and wished she had taken the thing off when she first saw Trish waiting for her, out there on the step.

But what good would that have done? It would only be another lie, to hide the major one. The one that Winona had said would bring truth.

And what truth?

Certainly not Ross Garrison's truth. Whenever Lynn tried to get near that, he cut her right off. She could still see him, the other night, his strong jaw clenched, staring straight ahead as he told her that he wasn't divorced, after all.

That his wife had *died*, for goodness sake.

Trish sat a little straighter. "Look. It's all right. You're engaged to him. And I just better get used to it. I know that. I do." Trish sniffed. "Mom's still mad—but she'll get over it. And don't get that doubtful look. She will. She always does. And besides, she…misses you. Just like me and Arlene do. We all keep getting in fights with each other, you know? Poor Clyde. We're drivin' him crazy. We get on each other's nerves. And you're not there. To settle us down. Now you're not around, it's pretty obvious to all of us, even if we don't like having to admit it, how much we really did count on you. And for more than just keeping things neat and tidy, you know?"

A feeling of lightness spread through Lynn. Maybe she'd never really reach Ross Garrison, but as far as her family went, things were looking up. "Oh, Trish…"

"I miss you, Lynnie."

"I miss you, too."

"We have to get over this stupid problem between us. We're a family, aren't we?"

"Yes. We certainly are."

"It's just like Papa always said…"

Lynn smiled to herself. Trish had always called Horace Taylor her "papa."

"You remember what he said, Lynnie? That family is more precious than diamonds or gold. And that we were a family, Papa and Mom, Arlene and you and me."

"Yes. I remember."

"Well, now Papa's gone. And I miss him. I really do."

"Me, too."

"But the rest of us, you and me and Mom and Leenie...we're still here. Still family. Aren't we?"

"Yes. Definitely. We are."

"It would be so wrong for us to forget that. For us to let stupid things, like who got the house—and who got a certain man—break us apart. We just can't let that happen."

"No. We can't."

"We won't, will we?"

"Absolutely not."

A single tear tracked its way down Trish's soft cheek. "I knew you would say that. But I'm sure glad to hear it, anyway."

The café curtains were open. For a moment Trish stared out at the backyard. Then she heaved a big sigh. "I need to get my own place." She looked back at Lynn. "No. I am not dropping hints that you should take me back here. It's time I found something just for myself. I know it won't be big. Something dinky is okay. As long as it's mine." She tipped her chin at a jaunty angle—a pose that betrayed the apprehension in her eyes. "I have to grow up someday, now, don't I?"

Softly Lynn asked, "Have you had any luck finding a new job?"

"Not yet. But I am trying. And I'm not gonna move—unless Clyde gets fed up and kicks me out—until I find one. I still have the money Papa left me, but I want my place to be something I pay for myself, something I *earned,* you know? I've been doing a lot of thinking lately, and it seems to me that a girl ought to earn her own way. Then, if the right fella ever does come along, well, I could be like you. Not depending on him to take care of me. Not *needing* him, you know? But just being with him because I wanted to, not because of something I could get from him."

It really did sound as if Lynn's baby sister had started to grow up. "Listen…" Lynn hesitated, still unsure if she was doing the right thing.

Green eyes bright and hopeful, Trish waited for her to go on.

Lynn took the leap. "There's a job opening up at the school.…"

Wednesday was Veterans' Day. Ross kept his office open. He had three early appointments: a new client seeking a divorce, one who wanted to make some changes to his will, and an adoption case. After that, there were the walk-ins: two land disputes and a Chapter Seven bankruptcy.

He and Mrs. Simms spent the remainder of the morning catching up on correspondence. She had his files in good order now. The office was spotless, everything in its place, tempting him to ask his new secretary if she'd ever considered cleaning houses in her spare time.

All through the morning, Lynn was never far from his mind. School would be closed today, wouldn't it? Would she be at home?

He hadn't contacted her since Saturday night, when she'd tried to pump him for details about Elana. That had really bothered him.

He was never going to discuss his wife with Lynn. It was bad enough that he'd told her the truth concerning his real beginnings. She hadn't needed to know about dear old Dad, the gambling, boozing womanizer, and Mom, the hopeless drunk.

But she had asked—and asked directly. There had been no way to get out of telling her, except to flatly refuse. And for some reason he himself didn't understand, he hadn't wanted to refuse her.

Still, he'd had to draw the line at the subject of Elana. His guilt and self-loathing on that score were his and his alone.

After he'd drawn that line, it had seemed wiser to keep away for a while, to give them both a little breather. Their "engagement" had been going on for over two weeks now. He'd bought her a ring, and they'd been seen together frequently. It wasn't going to rouse anyone's suspicions if they took a few days off from each other.

But unfortunately, he missed her. Way too much.

Dangerous. Damn dangerous, the way he couldn't seem to get her off his mind. Four or five times a day, at least, he had to stop himself from calling her. Sometimes he'd even gone so far as to pick up the phone and punch up the first two or three digits of her number.

But then he'd cut off the connection, thinking, *No. Wait. Give it a little more time....*

Were three and a half days enough?

They would have to be.

Because by noon on Wednesday, he'd decided they'd had enough damn time apart.

Chapter Twelve

The phone rang at five minutes past noon. Lynn's pulse started pounding; her breath caught in her throat.

She *knew* it would be him.

It was. "Lunch," he said.

"Right now?" Her heart lifted high in her chest, as if someone had just pumped it full of helium, enough to raise her feet right off the floor.

"I'm at the office. I'll pick you up. Ten minutes?"

"Okay." She hung up the phone and ran upstairs, where she changed her sweater twice, settling on one of the new ones, of course—teal-blue, with satin piping at the collar and on the sleeves. She freshened her makeup and fluffed up her hair.

When the doorbell rang, she literally flew down to answer it.

The sight of him standing there on her front step

banished all the ugly, sad doubts she'd been living with over the past few lonely days. Maybe she was a fool—a fool living a fool's dream.

But right then, a fool's dream was just fine with her.

They went to the State Street Grill. In a way, she'd started to think of the lovely, quiet restaurant as "their place." The food was excellent, and they enjoyed more privacy there than they did at the Hip Hop. And Ross said he liked to give the Grill his business. The restaurant was struggling a little, now that the summer season, with its modest tourist trade, had passed.

Through the meal, she kept thinking she should mention the other night, should at least try to achieve some sort of mutual acknowledgment with him concerning what had happened. That she'd broached a subject he considered forbidden, that he'd responded by cutting her off and then avoiding her for three days.

But every time she got her courage up to do it, she'd look across the table at him, see that gorgeous, rueful smile of his, the warmth and appreciation in his eyes. And she just couldn't do it. Couldn't ruin the moment. Couldn't bear to watch his jaw harden and his eyes turn cold.

So she told him of her progress with her family instead. That she and Trish had pretty much made peace, that Trish had an interview at the school for a new job, next Monday morning at nine. That she had called Arlene's again yesterday, and spoken to her stepmother.

"And?"

"She stayed on the line long enough to complain

about her blood pressure medicine. She thinks she wants to switch again. From a beta-blocker back to an ACE inhibitor.''

"Is that good?"

"Switching medicine? You'd have to ask her doctor about that."

"You know what I mean. That she stayed on the line to complain about the drugs she's taking."

"Yes. It is. Very good. It means she's well on the way to forgiving me."

His expression darkened. "*You're* not the one who needs forgiving, and you know it."

"I don't care who needs it. I sincerely do not. If my stepmother thinks *I* need it, fine. Whatever it takes."

He didn't agree with her. She could see that on his face. But he didn't argue further, and she appreciated that.

He kissed her when he dropped her off, a long, slow, sweet kiss, the kind that stole her breath and made her wish he'd never stop. When he lifted his head, she wanted to drag it back down again.

He said, "There's another dance at the Grange hall, this Saturday."

"Is that an invitation?"

"Pick you up at eight."

"I'll be ready."

"Lunch on Friday, too?"

"I'd love that."

He put her away from him and stepped back. "See you."

"Yes..."

And then he was gone.

* * *

Over the next week, she saw him five times. Three times for lunch, then for the dance at the Grange hall—and once, on Friday night, the twentieth, for a dinner date. They went to Bozeman that time, to a place that was famous for its Italian and French cuisine. Not once during any of those five dates did they discuss his deceased wife. They talked about how well his office was running now, about her students, about the weather, which had so far been mild. They flirted and teased each other—and scrupulously avoided opportunities to go any further than flirting.

Two or three times Lynn tried to lead them around to more intimate conversation. He always changed the subject—skillfully, yes, but she wasn't fooled.

His past life was off-limits.

More and more, she believed that his *heart* was off-limits, that no matter how hard she tried, he would never let her in.

And if that was the case, well, why did she keep kidding herself? They'd been on this whirlwind of lunches and dinners, of trips to Bozeman and Billings to sample French cuisine and visit movie houses, for almost a month now.

A month.

The length of time they'd agreed on when they started. Ironically, the lie they told *was* beginning to look like the truth. Not the engagement part of it. That remained a fake through and through.

But the other, about him not being the man for her. That had begun to look like nothing less than cold, hard fact.

She had wanted time, to reach out to him. Time to get him to show his true self to her.

Well, she had gotten her time. And she was getting nowhere.

Trish came to her classroom Monday, right after Lynn's students had left for the day. One glance at her sister's shining face and Lynn knew.

"Well?" she asked.

"I just talked to Mrs. Parchly."

"And?"

Trish let out a yelp of pure glee. "I got it." Trish flew across the room and threw her arms around Lynn's waist.

"Congratulations." Lynn held her sister's tiny body close, hugging back. Hard. "I'm so glad...."

"Me too. Oh, me too. Lynnie, I'm going to work really hard. I promise you. I'm going to learn this job and be good at it and make you proud."

"I *am* proud."

"Well." Trish pulled back, smoothed her hair and swiped at happy tears. "I am going to make you *prouder,* then. How's that?"

"Sounds wonderful to me."

Trish sniffed. "I've got to get back to the office. Mrs. Parchly is going to show me around a little, get me going on the paging and intercom system. Show me the ropes, you know?"

"Sounds exciting."

"Yeah. I'm nervous."

"You'll do just great."

"I hope so. Oh, and I almost forgot...."

"What?"

"Arlene asked me to see how you felt. About Thanksgiving?"

"Thanksgiving." Lynn glanced around her own

room, at the paper turkeys and Pilgrim hats, the cornucopia on the far wall, with a harvest of numbers and alphabet letters spilling out of it. Two more days to go. And then the four-day weekend. When class resumed on Monday, they'd start decorating for Christmas. Her students were already gearing up for the big annual Whitehorn Elementary Christmas Pageant, which would involve all the children at the school.

Time was definitely getting away from her.

Trish chewed her lower lip, clearly apprehensive. "Arlene said...well, she wants to ask you to come and have Thanksgiving with us. Or even, if you want to, we could have it at your house. We all kind of think it's time to let bygones be bygones. Even Mom. You know what she said yesterday?"

"Tell me."

"She said that Arlene should call you. That we shouldn't let the holidays go by without all of us together, the way Papa would have wanted it."

"I agree," Lynn said. "Either way—my house or Arlene's—would be just fine with me."

"You mean that?"

"I do."

"Arlene will call you, then. Tonight."

The phone rang at five. Lynn answered expecting to hear her older sister's voice.

But it was Ross. "How about dinner? At the Grill?"

Her kitchen calendar hung on the wall next to the phone. She stared at today's date: Monday November 23. Exactly one month since they'd become "engaged."

"Lynn? Are you still there?"

"Yes. Yes, I'm here."

"Will you have dinner with me?"

"I'd like that."

"About seven? I'll come for you."

She told him she'd be ready.

Arlene's call came fifteen minutes later. "Thanksgiving is coming," Lynn's older sister said rather stiffly, "and I think it's a good time to let bygones be bygones, don't you?"

Lynn smiled. "Yes, Arlene. I do."

"We all appreciate what you've done, finding Trish a new job."

"I'm glad I could help—and where shall we have our Thanksgiving dinner, your place or mine?"

"Well, I have been thinking about that. A lot. We *could* have it here, and that would be fine. But it would be nice to have it where we've always had it." Arlene's tone had softened, grown wistful. "It's kind of a family tradition, in a way. And you are so…organized. Things always seem to go better at your house. Sometimes I look around here and I wonder where all the mess comes from."

"Let's have it here."

Arlene drew a breath. "You're sure?"

"Positive."

"Well. All right, then. Let's do that. I've already got the turkey."

"You could bring it over Wednesday night."

"And you'll do those creamed onions? And the yams with marshmallows?"

"I will."

"And I'll get Mom to make the raspberry gelatin mold with cream cheese topping. And the pies…"

"Pumpkin *and* mince."

"Apple, too. I put up bread-and-butters *and* dills this year. And blackberry jam, for the rolls."

"I'm hungry already."

"Lynn?"

"Um?"

"Well, it's just…good to talk to you again, that's all."

"It's good to talk to *you.* How are you feeling?"

"Oh, what can I say? My ankles are too fat. And I get heartburn. It's probably better if you just don't get me started.…"

"Mother?"

"She's fine. She got the doctor to change her heart medicine. I'm sure you'll hear all about it. On Thursday. And I suppose…" Arlene paused to clear her throat. "I suppose you're going to want to invite that fiancé of yours."

Lynn's reply was automatic. "Yes, I do want to invite Ross." But in her heart, she couldn't help wondering, would he accept her invitation? Would they even still be "engaged" by then?

"All right," said Arlene, sounding resigned. "So Ross Garrison will be there."

"Yes." Lynn injected a good deal of assurance into the word. "And would you mind if I asked Danielle and Sara Mitchell, too? If they don't have plans, I mean. After all, it's just the two of them and—"

"You don't have to explain. Ask them."

"I will."

"And I'm…glad, that we're doing this."

Lynn agreed that she was, too.

Ross arrived right on time.

Lynn gestured him inside. "I'd like to speak with

you for a few minutes before we go.''

Dark eyes grew darker, with sheer wariness. He couldn't know about her Thanksgiving plans. But it wouldn't take a Princeton graduate to realize that the month of their "engagement" was drawing to a close.

He tried to skirt the inevitable with a stall. "I thought we'd agreed that it's not a good idea for me to come inside."

She suppressed a humorless laugh. "I promise, Ross. I won't try to seduce you."

"It's not you I'm worried about."

"I think you can control yourself, if you really put your mind to it."

"Lynn—"

"Please. I want to talk with you. In private. Now."

His reluctance achingly clear, he followed her into the living room. She went through the motions of offering him a chair, which he refused with an impatient shake of his dark head. "What is it?"

Fine. He didn't want to sit. She did. She sank to one of the two wing chairs, then cast about for a way to begin.

"I'm waiting," he said.

And scowling, too, she noted.

She decided to broach the easier subject first, though she knew it was only a stall of her own. If they ended up calling it off in the next few minutes, he wouldn't be coming to her family Thanksgiving anyway.

"I talked to Arlene tonight."

His scowl deepened. "You're saying you've made up with her, too. Is that it?"

"Yes. I have."

"Well, good. You wanted that pretty badly, didn't you? To make up with your family?"

"Yes. I wanted my family back." And I wanted more than that, she thought.

I wanted you.

His jaw was set, every line of his big body drawn taut. She wanted to reach out to him, to soothe him with a gentle touch.

She gripped the chair arms. "We've decided to have our family Thanksgiving here, at my house."

He looked at her for several seconds. Then he swore. "Thanksgiving dinner. Here? With your stepmother and Arlene...and Trish, too?"

"That's right."

He shoved his hands into the pockets of his fine wool slacks. "That's what this is about? You want me to come?"

"Yes. Very much."

He wasn't scowling anymore. Now he looked apprehensive—worse than apprehensive. He looked trapped.

He yanked one hand free of a pocket and shoved his fingers through his hair. "Damn it, Lynn..."

She did laugh then, a low, sad little chuckle. "I'm getting the feeling you're going to say no."

He looked down at the rug, over at the drapes that covered the front window—and finally, back at her. "Forgive me, but asking me to dinner with Jewel and Arlene and Trish...that sounds like a prescription for disaster if I ever heard one."

"It won't be a disaster, I can promise you that."

"Oh, come on. I know your stepsister."

She drew herself up in the chair. "Pardon me. But

you do not know my sister. Not really. And my family accepts the idea that I'm inviting you. They will be on their best behavior. So it will *not* be a disaster. It might not be a whole lot of fun. I admit that. But sometimes you have to do things in life that aren't particularly fun.''

He paced over to the window and remained there, facing away from her. She looked at his broad back, waited for him to turn to her again.

He didn't. He spoke to the drawn drapes. ''Listen. I've been thinking. Thanksgiving's a four-day weekend. Let's not waste it. Let's…get away.'' He did turn then, his expression both hopeful and bleak at the same time. ''We could fly to San Francisco. Or even Hawaii. I think I could arrange it. How would you like that? Four days on Maui?''

She shook her head, murmured his name.

He said something low and hard, under his breath, so she couldn't make it out. Then he strode toward her. He pulled himself up short a few feet from her chair. ''Don't look at me like that.''

''Like what?''

''As if I'm suggesting something impossible. We'd have separate rooms, if that's what you're worried about.''

She stared up at him. ''Why?''

''What do you mean, why? Why would we have separate rooms?''

''No, Ross. I mean, why in the world would we want to get away together? What purpose could that possibly serve? What we have isn't real, anyway. Is it?''

Ross glared down at her. He did look trapped. Yes. Trapped between what he wanted and what, for reasons she still didn't understand, he couldn't let himself have.

The time had come at last.

For the truth born of the lie.

She gave it to him. "I love you, Ross."

He muttered, "No." She felt as if something inside her was tearing, ripping a jagged wound in the center of her as he turned away once more. "No," he said again. In three long strides he was back at the curtained window, miles and miles away from her, showing her only the uncompromising line of his back.

She stood. And she dared to say it again, with more force. "I love you." He didn't move. He might have been carved from stone. She made herself go on. "I think I've loved you since the first. When you were my gentle, perfect prince for a night, when I knew there was more behind those cold eyes of yours than you let people see. I've…played this game with you. I've pretended, since you seemed to want it so much, that we were engaged. But not for the sake of anyone's reputation. Not for the sake of what people might say. I've learned that it's not really all that important, what people might say. I only—"

"Stop," he said on a rasping whisper.

She went on as if he hadn't spoken. "—wanted a little time. To try to find my way to you. To help you…find your way to me. And I got it, the time. But really, time hasn't taken us anywhere. We're both still pretending. What we share is not real, not…complete. You pick me up and you take me to dinner, we laugh and we joke, we talk about safe things. But it's not going anywhere. We're never alone together. We don't *dare* to be alone together.

We both know we can't afford that. We can't...make love again. It wouldn't be right.''

She waited, willing him to turn and face her. When he didn't, she muttered low, ''Ross. The time for pretending is up.''

He did turn then. His eyes were glacial, freezing her out.

She said very gently, ''We had an agreement. One month, and then it would end.''

She had him there, and they both knew it. His shoulders rose in a hopeless shrug.

And she couldn't hold back a cry. ''Oh, Ross. What is it? Why won't you take a chance with me? That's all I want. A chance to make this silly lie into the real thing. Please tell me, why won't you take that chance?''

But he didn't answer.

So she pressed on, into forbidden territory. ''Is it whatever happened with your wife?''

He muttered a low curse.

She took a step toward him. ''Ross...''

He put up a warding-off hand. ''Stop.'' He said it very clearly that time.

And she froze.

He swore again. She saw pain flare, a flash of heat in the coldness of those eyes. Pain. And something more. Something desolate. And hideously final.

He said. ''You want to know, do you? You *have* to know. About Elana.''

Somehow she made herself nod.

And he said, ''All right, then. I'll tell you.''

Chapter Thirteen

"Elana was beautiful," Ross said. "She had auburn hair and big brown eyes. When she walked into a room, every head would turn. I met her right after law school, a week before I went to interview with Turow, Travis and Lindstrom. I met her because I needed a good suit for that interview—and she sold me one."

Lynn ventured a question. "She worked in a men's clothing store?"

"She worked in the *best* men's clothing store in Denver. She was one of their top sales reps. I walked into that store and there she was, in a tight black skirt and matching jacket, looking…perfect. She took me by the arm. 'I'll take care of you,' she said. Then she put me together. That was how she said it. 'I'm going to put you together, Mr. Garrison.'

"She sold me a whole damn wardrobe that day.

A wardrobe I couldn't afford at the time. Suits and shirts, ties and shoes. Everything. And then she asked me out to lunch. By that weekend, we were lovers. And we'd found out that we…suited each other.''

Lynn sank to her chair again, murmuring, "You fell in love."

He gave her a distant look. "Love wasn't the issue. Neither of us was looking for that. Or at least, I wasn't.''

Lynn's disbelief must have shown on her face. He answered the question he saw in her eyes. "Yes, all right. I said the words. I *told* her I loved her. And she said she loved me. But the words weren't that important. Just something people say. We were right for each other, saw the potential in each other. The way I viewed it, we were partners. Partners who trusted and respected each other. We would treat each other right and work together for our future.

"She came from a poor family, just like me. From some little town in Arkansas. She grew up in a double-wide, with a drunk for a mother and a father who was never there. Just like me. She told me she'd been looking for the right man, to take her where she wanted to go. And guess what? She'd found him— me.

"We were married a month after we met. And she was everything I expected her to be. We had four houses as I clawed my way up through the firm. She decorated all of them, with an eye for color and detail that had the other wives in the firm green with envy. She was always the life of the party, too. Charming and funny. And sexy enough to strike sparks off a dead man.

"By the time I was twenty-eight and made partner,

I thought I had it all. Thought I had *earned* it all—
with the help of my perfect wife. That we'd both
gotten what we wanted—the good life. Success. My
mama might have spent her life staring into the bottom of a bottle of rotgut whiskey. My daddy might
have gotten his brains blown out all over a jealous
husband's bed. But I had arrived. I had *made* it.''

He paused, took a deep and ragged breath.

She waited, hardly daring to breathe herself.

Finally he went on. ''What I didn't know was that
she had *helped* me in ways I hadn't realized. Because
there wasn't a man in the firm who didn't want her.
And she had…struck a few deals of her own. She
had slept with my supervisors, with more than one
of the partners. And after she slept with them, I got
promoted.''

Lynn must have made some sound of distress. He
turned a hard glare on her. ''You wanted to hear this.
Don't interrupt.''

Lynn pressed her lips together, gave a tight nod.

He laughed, the sound as cold as a midwinter's
night. ''What is it people say? The husband is always
the last to know? Well, I was. The last to know. I'd
been a partner for almost three years when the word
finally got around to me. I went home that night, to
my perfect wife in our beautiful house—and threw
up. And then I confronted her. She must have had
some inkling the ax was about to fall, because she
was drinking, had *been* drinking, through most of the
afternoon, even though, as a rule, she never had more
than one or two cocktails a couple of nights a week.
I started shouting at her. Accusations. She poured
herself another drink, tried to stay calm. At first.

''She'd done it for my sake, she said, to help me

advance. When I called her a liar, she admitted there might have been more. There might have been just a little bit of revenge in it for her. Because I had never loved her. She knew I had never loved her. For years, she said, I'd hardly known she was there. I expected her to *perform,* she said, and that was all I wanted from her. To keep my house for me and give good parties and entertain my colleagues. And so she *had* entertained them. In spades. She had given me what I really wanted. She'd seen to it that I made partner, and that I did it fast.

"After she laid all that on me, I shouted even louder. I don't even remember all the names that I called her. All I remember is how much I despised her then. How just looking at her sickened me. To my mind, *we* had been partners, the two of us. I had trusted her, believed we were building something together. And she had betrayed me. Put me in my place. Son of a drunk and a wife-stealing gambler...whose own wife was no better than a whore.

"In the end, she grabbed her purse and ran out the front door. I heard her car start up and roar away down the drive. I sat down and I stared at the wall. For a long time. Hours. Finally I dragged myself off to bed."

He was back at the drawn drapes again, staring at them as if he could see right through them.

"I didn't wake up until a little after 2:00 a.m. When there was a knock on the door. The Denver police. They wanted me to come to the morgue and identify her body. That fourth house we had was on top of a steep hill. She'd gone over the cliff on her way down."

Lynn wanted to stand, to go to him. But he

turned—and he stared at her, a stare that froze her in her chair.

He said, "Why the hell are you crying?"

She blinked, felt the wetness, on her cheeks, running down her chin. "I don't…" She gulped back a sob. "Oh, Ross. I'm so sorry. For you. And for her…"

"Don't be," he said harshly. "Not for me, anyway. Elana was right about me. I never did love her. I used her. And that change I said I wanted, the reason I moved here to Whitehorn? Well, I wanted a change, all right. I wanted to get as far away as possible from Denver and from Turow, Travis and Lindstrom—where half of the partners had slept with my dead wife."

Lynn brought up both hands, smeared the tears off her cheeks. Then she forced herself to rise. "Ross. Please…"

He shook his head, a savage gesture, quick and ruthless as the slashing of a knife. "No." He chopped the air with a hand. "God. You are amazing. You are…everything I ever secretly hoped might be somewhere in the world. Look at you. Standing there. Crying. For me. You are, aren't you? You're crying for me?" It was an accusation.

She saw no need to answer it. He was right. She cried for him. And for the woman he had married. For two people who had needed love so desperately, and had never had anyone to show them how to find it.

"Save your tears, Lynn. Save them for someone who deserves them."

She swiped at her cheeks again. "Oh, Ross. I think you do deserve them."

"No," he said. "I don't. And you were right. You said I've been pretending. And I have. Pretending what might have been. If I was someone different. If I'd met you sooner. But I didn't meet you sooner. And now, you're right about the rest of it, too. The month is up. And you have just learned why I'm not the man for you."

She opened her mouth to form the word *no*.

He didn't give her a chance to utter it. "I'm no prince," he said. "You can see that now."

"It doesn't matter. Oh, Ross. It's…only the past. It can haunt you. And hurt you. But what really matters is who you are, what you do, how you live right now. What matters is that you've told me the things you thought you had to keep secret. And that I don't hate you for them. I only…understand you better. Can't you see? My love is still here. Still yours. And if you could love me in return…"

He made a low, cruel, scoffing sound. "But that's the point, Lynn. That's exactly the point."

"What? I don't—"

"The point is, I haven't got a clue what love is."

Those words struck her like blows. She could see in his eyes that he really believed them.

And that anything she said right then would fall on deaf ears.

But maybe, with a little time…

Lord. There she went again. Thinking that time would do it, when it hadn't, up till now. Thinking that her love was magic, as sweet old Winona Cobbs had promised her. That all she had to do was believe in it and it wouldn't let her down.

Well, she had believed in it. With all her heart and soul.

Too bad *he* didn't believe in it.

One last tear brimmed over her lower lid. Very deliberately, she wiped it away. "All right. Wait there, please. I won't be a minute."

He was standing in the same place, a few feet from the wing chair, when she came back down the stairs. "Here are your rings." She held out the small black velvet case.

He glowered at her, insulted. "I don't want them."

"Neither do I."

She kept her hand extended until he reached out and took the case. He stuck it in a pocket.

She gave him a last smile. "Come on. I'll walk you to the door."

Chapter Fourteen

Lynn called Danielle after Ross left. She invited her friend to her family Thanksgiving. But Danielle had already told the McCallums that she and Sara would join them at their house.

"And what's the matter?" Danielle asked. "You sound strange."

So Lynn told her that she and Ross wouldn't be getting married, after all.

Danielle was sweet and sympathetic. She stayed on the phone with Lynn for over an hour, saying all the things a friend will say: *It will work out* and *I'm here. Anytime you need me. All you have to do is call....*

Lynn felt a little better by the time she hung up.

Arlene brought the turkey over on Wednesday night. She and Lynn prepared the stuffing, standing side by side at the kitchen counter, while Arlene's two children, Darla Sue and Bobby Clyde, watched television in the other room.

Arlene talked nonstop as they diced celery and chopped giblets. She said she was gaining more weight with this baby than she had with the other two, that Clyde was working way too many hours, driving to Billings and back every day, to sell farm machinery out of the dealership he ran there. She never saw him. And she worried that maybe he was staying out of the house on purpose. That living with his pregnant wife, their two children, Arlene's mother *and* Arlene's baby sister was just a little more than he could take.

Lynn reminded her sister that her husband adored her. That Trish did plan to move out soon—and hadn't Arlene and Clyde been talking about getting a bigger house?

Yes, Arlene admitted. Trish would be moving out. And a bigger house was in the offing. That was the good thing about Clyde working so much. They did have the money to move.

"But sometimes," Arlene said with a sigh, "I look in the mirror—at my fat stomach and my ratty hair. I look around at my house, where there's always a mess. And I just wish…well, I almost wish I could go back. Be where you are now. Engaged and thin." She sighed again. "Yes. That's the perfect time in a woman's life. She's got a ring on her finger, but she's still got her figure—which reminds me…"

Lynn knew what was coming.

And it was. "Trish told me about that ring of yours."

Lynn didn't reply, only scooped up olives in both

hands and dumped them in the big bowl full of dressing.

Arlene stirred the olives in and asked very gently, "Lynnie, where is your ring? Why haven't you shown it to me?"

"Because I gave it back." Lynn turned to the sink, flipped on the faucet and rinsed her hands.

The big wooden spoon Arlene was using stopped in midswipe. "Oh, Lynnie...no."

Lynn grabbed a towel, wiped her hands. "It didn't work out, that's all." She hung the towel back on its hook.

Arlene dropped the spoon into the bowl. She rubbed her hands down her apron, then held out her arms. "C'mon. Come here."

Lynn let her sister hold her. It was an awkward proposition, with Arlene's stomach between them. Arlene made little crooning sounds and patted Lynn's back.

Finally she took Lynn by the arms and pushed her away enough that she could look into Lynn's eyes. "What happened? Tell me everything."

Lynn shook her head. "I'd really rather not go into it. We broke up Monday night. He just..." She remembered the explanation that she and Ross had agreed on and decided it would work as well as any. "It turned out he wasn't the right man for me."

"You're sure?"

Lynn nodded.

"This isn't just a lovers' spat?"

"No. It's over. It really is."

"Well." Arlene let go of Lynn. Her look of concern turned to something of a sneer. "I have to say it. *I* never liked him."

"Arlene…"

"Oh, no, you don't."

"What?"

"You're defending him."

"I'm *not* defending him."

"Oh, yes, you are. And even if you won't tell me exactly what happened, I can guess."

"Arlene, please. Don't go jumping to conclusions. There's no one to blame here. All that happened, honestly, is that it didn't work out."

"Well, of course you're going to say that. We all know how you are. You wouldn't say mean things about the devil himself."

"Arlene—"

"Just tell me this much. Who broke up with who?"

"*I* broke up with him."

"No."

"Yes."

"I don't believe that."

"Well, too bad. It's true."

"Your heart is broken. I can see that."

"My heart is just fine." Now, there was a lie. But Lynn knew her sisters and her stepmother. She didn't want them taking up residence at the Hip Hop, spreading tales about Ross.

Arlene went to the table, yanked out a chair and sank into it. "Oh, Lord…" Her breath came in sharp little pants, the way it sometimes did when she was pregnant and something had upset her. "Oh, my…"

Lynn went to her. "Arlene, please don't get yourself worked up. You know it's not good for you, or for the baby."

"But I was just getting used to the idea that you would marry him. And now this…"

"We'll get through it."

Arlene started sniffling.

"Arlene. Don't…"

But there was no stopping Arlene once she got going. The tears came flooding out. "Oh, just look at me," Arlene sobbed. "Why am *I* crying? *You* should be crying. I love my babies, the good Lord knows I do. But I *hate* being pregnant. Fat as a big old she-bear. And blubbering over every little thing…"

Lynn knelt enough to embrace Arlene's slim shoulders. "It's all right. Really…"

"Oh, my. Oh, Lord," Arlene moaned against Lynn's shirt. "Trish said it was such a pretty ring. That the diamond was two whole carats, at least. And I was already starting to think about your wedding, you know? Starting to look forward to helping you choose just the right dress. It was going to be such fun. I was going to make it all up to you, for the rotten things I said, for the mean, awful way we all acted when we found out about you and that man.…"

There was a box of tissues on the table. Lynn yanked out a couple and put them in Arlene's hand. "Arlene. Calm down now.…"

Arlene sniffed and dabbed at her eyes. "I don't care what you say. I *hate* that Ross Garrison. First he dangled Trish along. And then he—"

"Arlene. I mean it." Lynn stood up straight and put steel in her tone. "I don't want you bad-mouthing Ross Garrison. The truth is, he was never interested in Trish. Trish admits that now. And as for me, he treated me…like a princess. He truly did. And *I* was the one who broke up with him.''

''But—''

''I want your solemn promise, Arlene. I want you to swear to me that you won't say bad things about him.''

Arlene loosed a low, rather pitiful whine. ''Oh, Lynnie.'' She honked into a tissue. ''You were always such a good person. I have to admit it. Sometimes it really irritates me, how good you are.''

''I want your promise, Arlene. I mean it. I do.''

Arlene sniffed and blew her nose again. ''Oh, Lynnie.''

''Promise. Come on.''

''Oh, all right. I won't say a word about him. I'll keep my mouth shut. But don't expect me to like it.''

''Thank you.''

Arlene let out a final unhappy moan. ''You are too good to live, you know that?'' With a grunt of discomfort, she pushed herself from the chair. ''Come on. Let's get that darn bird stuffed.''

Lynn had the table set when the family arrived the next day. Her sisters and Jewel told her it was beautiful. Through the afternoon and evening, they never missed an opportunity to praise her, to hug her, to pat her arm tenderly, to show her in a thousand ways that they loved her and only wanted to put what had happened in the past behind them for good.

Both Jewel and Trish found their own opportunities to let Lynn know just what they thought of Ross Garrison. Lynn made it as clear to them as she had to Arlene: they were to leave the man alone.

Grudgingly, they agreed that they wouldn't say

rude things about the lawyer to anyone but each other. They wouldn't defame him with the good citizens of Whitehorn. But what they said in the privacy of the family, well, Lynn would just have to put up with that. They wouldn't say those things to her, if she didn't want to hear them. But they had a right to their own opinions, now, didn't they?

Lynn sighed and decided to leave it at that.

When they sat down to eat, Clyde said the prayer. Lynn looked up after the amens and saw the moisture in Jewel's eyes. Lynn knew her stepmother was thinking of her father. Until they had lost him, Horace had always said the Thanksgiving prayer.

After dinner they all worked together to get the dishes rinsed and stacked. Then they sat in the living room chatting, watching the children play with the toys that Lynn kept for them in a trunk in the corner, giving the huge meal a chance to settle a little before they tackled the pies. Then, after dessert, they gathered around the upright piano that had once belonged to Lynn's mother. Lynn played and they sang the old Thanksgiving hymns, "Harvest Home" and "For the Beauty of the Earth." From there they progressed to children's songs, so that Bobby Clyde and Darla Sue could join in, too.

The family left at a little after eight, bearing most of the leftover food in plastic containers and on foil-wrapped platters.

"It was lovely," said Jewel.

Lynn's sisters and brother-in-law chorused their agreement.

There was a last flurry of hugs and then they were gone.

Lynn went back to the kitchen and finished cleaning up. Then she sat in the breakfast nook with a hot cup of tea and looked at the phone for a while.

She didn't pick it up.

But she wanted to. Oh, sweet Lord, how she wanted to....

In the big log house on Black Bear Lake, Ross sat alone in front of the fire. There was a phone on the end table, a few inches from his hand.

About now, he thought, that impossible family of Lynn's would have gone home. She'd be alone.

Doing what? Maybe sitting at that little table in the kitchen. Or watching TV. Or perhaps she'd already climbed the stairs to her room.

What did it look like, her room?

Hell if he knew.

They'd had a month together. A whole damn month.

And he'd never seen where she slept.

And that was a good thing. He should look at it that way.

He'd taken her innocence. Messed up her life. Wrecked things with her family.

But he'd done what he could to rectify the wrongs he'd done her. He'd stood by her when she needed him. And he'd managed to keep himself from taking her to bed again.

She even had that annoying family of hers back now.

He didn't see how that family was anything to get excited over. But she had wanted them. And now she had them.

And they *would* have gone home by now.

Wouldn't they?

Which brought him back to his original question. What was she doing right now?

He moved his hand. Only a few inches. It settled onto the smooth black body of the phone. He picked it up. The dial tone hummed in his ear.

"No," he said aloud, and set it back down.

Lynn called Danielle first thing the next morning. Danielle answered with a cheery hello and Lynn said, "I was wondering, have you had breakfast yet?"

"As a matter of fact, Sara is just pouring her cornflakes all over her place mat."

"Well, tell her to scoop up those cornflakes and put them back in the box. I want you two to meet me at the Hip Hop. For breakfast."

"My, my. Feeling ready to face any challenge, are we?"

"I need to get out. I need...cheering up. And everyone will know about Ross and me by now, anyway."

"You're sure?"

"Yep. I want a short stack, sausage and two over easy. And I want someone else to cook it for me."

"Okay, then. I'll be there. The Hip Hop. In twenty minutes?"

"Done."

Lily Mae and Winona were waiting. Lily Mae's bracelets jangled as she waved Lynn over. They insisted that Lynn sit with them at their table, and pulled more chairs up when Danielle and her daughter arrived.

Lynn told the two older women frankly that she and Ross had changed their plans. There would be no wedding, after all.

Lily Mae's false eyelashes fluttered. "Oh, now, honey. What did that Shakespeare fella say? 'The course of true love is one rocky road.' Or something like that. You will work it out. I just know you will."

Lynn chose not to argue the point. Maybe she was hoping, just a little, that Winona would say something.

Something mystical. Something meaningful.

Something to allow her to imagine that Lily Mae might be right.

But Winona had no psychic pronouncements to make that particular morning. She only smiled and asked Lynn to pass her a couple of individual creamers.

"I've managed to cut out the sugar," she said. "But I just can't get along without my cream."

Lynn went to her empty classroom later in the day. She took down the Thanksgiving decorations and got out the materials for the first of the Christmas projects. In the afternoon, Trish called to invite her to Arlene's for dinner.

She went. She got home at nine, took a long bath and went to bed. She stared at the shadowed ceiling for a long time, thinking of what might have been.

Wishing...

But no. Somehow, she would get over Ross.

One day, one hour, one minute at a time.

It snowed on Monday, the first snowfall of the season. Big, sloppy wet flakes that didn't stay long on the ground. Ross looked out the window of his office, saw it falling—and thought of Lynn.

Pictured her. Standing out in the schoolyard with her students, laughing, tipping her face up...

He reached for the phone. He knew she wouldn't be home. But maybe she'd bought that new answering machine by now. He could call.

And what?

Listen to the sound of her recorded voice asking for a message he had no intention of leaving?

He swore and yanked his hand back, as if the phone could burn him. Then he got up and closed the blinds so he wouldn't have to keep imagining her with her head tipped back and snowflakes melting on her tongue.

Tuesday, the sky was clear. Ross got up in the morning and looked at the scummy rim in his big bathtub and decided to stay home until he'd talked to his housekeeper. When she came in, he fired her.

Then he went to work and asked Mrs. Simms if she could recommend anyone to clean his house for him.

Mrs. Simms said, "As it so happens, I have a cousin who runs her own little service."

Ross called the cousin. He met her at his house that evening at five. A solid, iron-haired, no-nonsense woman in overalls, a flannel shirt and heavy work boots. She looked around the great room and declared, "Mr. Garrison, you need help here."

They struck a bargain. She would start Thursday at seven in the morning.

He came home Thursday evening to a spotless house—and Lynn's red shoe, perched daintily atop a scrap of notepaper on the kitchen counter.

The sight of that shoe almost finished him off. His briefcase slid from his hand, dropping to the floor with a dull thud.

And that first night came flooding back to him.

The red dress sprinkled with stardust. The sound of her laughter. The dancing bubbles in a glass of champagne.

And later. When he'd carried her up the stairs to his room. The shoe slipping off her foot, hitting the stairs as it bounced down behind them.

And later still, in his room, where she had called him her Prince for a Night.

A torn laugh escaped him.

Prince for a night.

Carefully he reached out and nudged the shoe off the scrap of paper. He leaned closer, so that he could read the words written there in his housekeeper's neat, square hand.

"Mr. Garrison, I found this shoe wedged in that little crawl space under the stairs. It looks like a good one. The owner will probably want it back."

He stared at the shoe again.

A week. A damn, interminable week he had stayed away from her. And he'd fully intended to stay away forever.

To see her would be hell.

But Mrs. Simms's cousin was right. Lynn did want her shoe back. She had asked him more than once if he knew what had happened to it.

What choice did he have?

The damn thing had to be returned.

Chapter Fifteen

"So we get to have *wings,* Miss Taylor," Sara said. "Wings and long white dresses. Like nightgowns."

"Just gowns," Jenny corrected her friend. "That's what they call them. Angel gowns."

"Yes," agreed Sara. "Jenny's right. Angel gowns. Everybody in the chorus gets one. Our moms have to make them—and the wings, too. And Jenny and me, we get special wings. With extra gold sparkles on them, because we have to do a duet."

"That's what it's called." Jenny's yellow curls bounced as she nodded her head. "A duet. When two people sing together. Like me and Sara get to do for the Christmas pageant."

"So you have to *picture* it, Miss Taylor," Sara instructed. "In the multipurpose room, up on the stage, with all the pretty decorations all around. And all the kids in the chorus, the *angel* chorus, standing in rows in their angel gowns and their angel wings. And then me and Jenny step forward. Real slow. Real...floaty-like, the way angels would. Are you picturing it?''

Lynn folded her hands on her desk and smiled at the two little girls, who had stayed after school to rehearse their parts for the Christmas pageant. ''I am. I can just see it....''

Sara and Jenny looked at each other. Identical grins bloomed on cherubic faces.

''I think she can,'' said Sara.

''Me, too,'' said Jenny. She glanced toward the windows that faced the playground. ''Oh, look. It's snowing.''

Two pairs of blue eyes widened in delight.

''I hope it *keeps* snowing,'' Sara declared. ''I hope it snows and snows and we can have a white Christmas. That's the best kind.''

''And then we can build a snowman,'' said Jenny, ''with sticks for arms and a carrot for a nose and a—''

''Girls,'' Lynn warned. ''Stay on task.''

Both girls sighed and faced Lynn again. As one, they stepped forward, leaving the rest of the imaginary chorus behind.

''We're going to sing our duet for you now,'' said Sara with great dignity.

''I'm all ears,'' said Lynn.

The two girls looked at each other and giggled. ''It's just an expression,'' said Sara to Jenny.

''I know that,'' said Jenny, and the two giggled again.

''Come on,'' said Lynn. ''Let me hear it. We don't

have much time.'' She glanced at the clock. ''Eight minutes, and then you have to be at your rehearsal.''

''We know,'' the girls chirped in unison. They both drew their shoulders back, tipped their cute chins upward. Their high, clear voices trilled out.

''In the winter, in a manger, in a stable dark and drear.

There's a sweet baby sighing. Listen. Can you hear?

There's a donkey and lambkin, a shepherd and three kings.

A mother and father and the one of whom we—''

Three short, hard raps on the door cut the song short.

Sara stomped her foot. ''Oh, who's that? We were just getting to the good part.'' She frowned at Jenny. ''And you messed up again. At that high part, the three kings part.''

Jenny looked down at her shoes. ''I know. I'm not as good as you. But I'm gonna work on it. I really am.''

Sara relented and patted her friend's shoulder. ''That's all right. You're gonna do fine. We have plenty of time to get it right.''

''It's just beautiful.'' Lynn was already out of her chair and halfway to the door. ''And you two had better go on and get into your coats now.''

''But Miss Taylor.'' Sara put on her most pitiful expression. ''You haven't heard the whole thing.''

''You can sing it for me Monday.'' Lynn grasped the door handle and spoke over her shoulder at the girls. "Or Tuesday." She pushed open the door, then turned to greet her visitor. "I promise we'll find the time to—" The words died in her throat. There was only one word right then. It filled up her mind, her heart, her classroom, the world: "Ross."

He said something. Probably hello. But her heart was booming so loud, and her mind was a whirlwind. Every last bit of saliva seemed to have dried right up inside her mouth. All she could do was whisper his name. Again.

"Ross…"

"Hello, Lynn." His voice. Deep. Rich. Too well remembered…

He was real. Standing there in the shadows of the outside hall between the classrooms. Holding a shopping bag, wearing dark slacks, a charcoal-colored sweater and a heavy, gorgeous camel hair coat. Snowflakes clung to his broad shoulders, gleaming silver-white.

"That's my lawyer," Jenny announced from her spot near the front of the room.

"I know he's a lawyer," said Sara. "My mom told me."

"Hi, Mr. Garrison!" Jenny called brightly.

The air outside was very cold. Lynn shook herself. What a fool. Standing here gaping at him, with the door open.

"Come in," she said. He did. She shut the door.

She turned to her students. "Come on, now. Coats, hats and mittens. Just leave your packs in the nook. You can get them later." She clapped her hands. "Double time. You don't want to be late, do you?"

That got the girls moving. They darted for the coat nook. Lynn watched them, suddenly unwilling to turn back to the man who stood behind her. Blond curls bouncing, the two little angels disappeared beyond the open doorway. She could hear them. Giggling together—and probably slipping on each other's winter jackets, switching mittens and mufflers and bright wool hats, too.

"Lynn."

The sound of her name on his lips turned her inside out. Her silly knees felt like water. And her heart went on thudding, hammering out her foolish, hopeless longing against the wall of her chest.

She turned to him. "I have to take Sara and Jenny to the multipurpose room."

"That's all right. I can wait."

As he spoke, there was another tap at the door. He turned and opened it.

It was Mrs. Parchly, wrapped up in a plaid coat, a trailing purple muffler under her chin and a stack of bright red papers in her mittened hand. Lynn ushered the secretary inside and performed the introductions.

"Oh, yes," said Mrs. Parchly. "You're the lawyer, the one Trish used to work for?"

"That's me."

"She's a good little worker, isn't she? It must have been hard to let her go." Ross made a noise in his throat, which the older woman apparently took as agreement. She turned a big smile on Lynn. "Actually, I'm giving her a chance to handle the desk by herself." She peeled off a handful of the flyers she was carrying. "These are about the winter food drive. I could have left them in your box, I know. But Trish needs the practice, working on her own. And I like to get out and walk around, especially this

time of day, right after lunch, when your kindergartners have gone home and the other students are all
back in their classrooms. It's so nice and quiet in the
halls.''

"I know what you mean." Lynn took the flyers
just as the girls emerged, still giggling, from the coat
nook. As expected, they had switched jackets. Lynn
gave them a patient look. "Ready?"

"Yes, Miss Taylor," said Jenny.

"And we better hurry," Sara warned.

"And where are you two going?" asked Mrs.
Parchly. "Rehearsal, I'll bet."

"Yes," said Sara with great importance. "It's a
private rehearsal, fifteen whole minutes with just me
and Jenny and Mr. Beals, the director."

Mrs. Parchly glanced at Lynn. "Would you like
me to walk them over?"

"We gotta get *going*," Sara insisted.

"It's no problem at all," said Mrs. Parchly.

Lynn murmured a thank-you as Sara shoved open
the door. "Come *on*. We gotta go."

Mrs. Parchly laughed. "An eager little beaver, that
one." She gave Ross a quick nod. "Nice to meet
you."

He dipped his dark head in response.

The secretary followed the girls outside. The door
swung shut behind them.

And Lynn was left there, clutching her stack of
flyers, her mouth dry and her heart aching.

Alone with Ross.

Questions tumbled all over themselves in her head.
Why had he come here? Dare she hope he had
changed his mind? Was he ready to *believe?* Ready
to accept her love?

The way he was looking at her—so intently. So…hungrily. As if he wanted to eat her right up.

That was good, wasn't it?

A sign that he had missed her? An indication that he—

The rest of that question flew right out of her head when he said, "I hired a new housekeeper."

"A…new housekeeper?" she parroted. It wasn't at all what she'd hoped he might say.

"She's very thorough."

"Well. That's good. Isn't it?"

"She found this. Under the stairs." He extended his hand.

The shopping bag. He was trying to give her the shopping bag he had brought in with him.

She set the stack of flyers on a nearby desk and took the bag.

"Open it."

Ross watched her as she carefully peeled the sides apart and peered inside. How would she react, he wondered, if he grabbed the damn bag back, tossed it away and pulled her into his arms?

God, how he wanted that, to feel her against him. To taste her sweet mouth again, to take off her fluffy green sweater and her pencil-thin skirt and make love to her. He wanted to lay her down, right there, next to that stack of bright red flyers, on the nearest group of child-sized desks, which were pushed together in a semicircle just a few feet away.

Yes. He wanted to make love to her, *needed* to make love to her. Now. With that row of paper Santas grinning down at them from a nearby bulletin board. He wanted, he *needed* to bury himself in her, and damn the price, damn whoever might walk in on them. Let that secretary poke her head in and see them. He didn't care....

She looked up. That sweet mouth was trembling. "Oh, Ross. My shoe? Is that all you came for—to give me back my shoe?"

Lynn knew it was more than that. It *had* to be more than that. She could see it in his eyes, see how he wanted her. How he was keeping himself from reaching for her. His mouth was a grim, determined line. And he held his fists clenched, white-knuckled, at his sides.

He said her name, "Lynn..." in longing and complete confusion.

She let out a cry, dropped the bag to the floor and threw herself against him, lifting her mouth.

He covered it, yanking her close, letting out a starved, needful moan of his own, one that sang through her body as his arms closed around her.

He kissed her as if he would die if he didn't. Joy seared through her, zinging along every nerve. She slid her hands up, over the lush wool of his coat, feeling the wetness of melting snowflakes, cold on his shoulders.

She encircled his neck, pressed herself into him. His tongue swept her mouth. His hands clasped her waist and slid up, under her sweater. She quivered, cried out again.

He murmured, "We can't...it's not right..." against her mouth.

And she sighed. "I know...."

Everything changed then, in the space of those few cryptic shared words.

He smoothed her sweater carefully back in place

and guided her head to his shoulder. For a moment he just held her, the embrace all tenderness now.

And she gloried in that tenderness, drank it into herself, just as she had his savage, needful kiss seconds before. She might have stood there forever, cradled in his arms, listening to his heartbeat, to the ragged sound of his breath sighing in and out of his chest.

But the sweet moment didn't last long.

It was shattered when the door flew back behind them and Jenny McCallum burst into the room.

"Miss Taylor, Miss Taylor!" The child was gasping for breath, her cherub's face dead white. "Bad men grabbed Sara. You've got to come quick!"

Chapter Sixteen

Jenny flew to Lynn's side and grabbed for her hand. "Hurry, hurry. We have to stop them. They're going to hurt Sara, and there's a lady, she's already hurt. She's just lying there, on the cold ground. Oh, please, Miss Taylor. Hurry up now!"

"Where?" demanded Ross. "Jenny, where are those 'bad men'?"

"In the parking lot. Mrs. Parchly was taking too long and Sara and me decided to go by ourselves and—" She let out a frantic cry and yanked on Lynn's hand. "I can't 'splain it all now." She gave a low, terrified whimper. "We have to save Sara. We have to hurry—"

Right then, Mrs. Parchly appeared in the open doorway. "Jenny, there you are. I turned my back for a moment and—where's Sara? Oh, this is so upsetting. I had to make one stop, that's all. I told the girls to stay with me, but they—''

''Excuse me,'' said Ross. He cut around the secretary.

''What is going on here?'' demanded Mrs. Parchly as Ross rushed past her. ''Where is Sara? Will someone please—''

But there was no time to answer Mrs. Parchly's questions, and Jenny knew it. ''Come on, with my lawyer,'' the child begged, still dragging at Lynn's hand. ''We have to go now!''

They ran out together, following Ross, Jenny leading Lynn, Mrs. Parchly falling in behind.

''This way, this way,'' Jenny kept chanting. ''Hurry. This way…''

They emerged from the shadowed open hall between the buildings. Save for the few rows of cars and the steadily falling snow, the parking lot appeared deserted.

''They've gone!'' Jenny cried out. ''The bad men took Sara and ran away!''

''What?'' Mrs. Parchly blanched. ''Bad men? What bad men? Oh, my heavens, what is going on here?''

Ross stopped at the edge of the walkway and turned back to Jenny. ''You said there was a lady…?''

Jenny pointed. ''Over there.''

They fled together in that direction, off the curb and onto the blacktop.

A few feet from the row of cedar trees that rimmed the outer edge of the lot, between a beat-up SUV that belonged to one of the teachers and another car Lynn didn't recognize, they found the woman. She was lying faceup on the blacktop, unconscious. The snow had yet to start building up on the ground. But it clung to her pale, pretty face, gleaming silver-white in her dark hair, dusting her brows, catching in the crease between her soft lips.

"That's her. That's the lady!" cried Jenny.

"My goodness," Mrs. Parchly gasped. "That's Mrs. Sheppard...."

Lynn had never seen the woman before. "Who?"

"A new teacher. She was just in to see Mrs. Taggert for a final interview. Oh, my Lord, what is happening here?"

Ross was already shrugging out of his coat and tucking it around the still form on the ground. He pressed two fingers to the woman's white throat. "Her pulse is steady." With great care, he used his thumb to raise one of the woman's eyelids. "Out cold," he said. "We'd better not try to move her." He slid a hand inside his jacket and pulled out a cell phone. Flipping it open, he punched up a number.

Lynn stood beside Mrs. Parchly, clutching little Jenny's hand and shivering without her coat, as Ross called an ambulance and then the sheriff's office.

Once he'd made the calls, he beckoned Jenny. She let go of Lynn's hand and went to him. Still crouching, so that his eyes and Jenny's could meet on a level, he clasped her mittened hands. "Did you see which way the bad men went?"

"No. Oh, no. One of them grabbed Sara by the back of her jacket...I mean, by *my* jacket...I mean—"

"It's okay. Settle down. Tell me slowly."

"I...um...Sara and me came out from the hall and saw the bad men. They were fighting with the lady."

"How many bad men?"

"Two."

"Have you ever seen either of those men before?"

"I don't know. I couldn't tell. They had on those mask hats, like you wear when you're skiing?"

"Ski masks over their faces, is that what you're saying?"

Jenny nodded.

"Okay. Then what happened?"

"One of them pushed the lady. She hit her head on the car and fell down. Sara got mad then. She started running toward them, shouting at them to leave that poor lady alone. Then the men started coming after us. Sara said, 'Uh-oh. We better run.'

"So we ran. Back the other way. But Sara was behind me then. And one of them caught her. I wanted to go help her, but Sara screamed at me to hurry, get away and get help. I ran. I didn't look back until I got to our classroom. I...didn't see where they went." The sweet face started to crumple. "I don't know where they went. I didn't turn around again. I didn't see. I only ran. I should've looked, shouldn't I?"

Ross held Jenny's hands more tightly and stared hard into her eyes. "Jenny. Listen to me. You did just the right thing." He looked up at Lynn and gestured with a quick toss of his dark head.

She hurried to the child, gathered her up in her arms. Those small mittened hands closed around her neck. "I should have looked...." Jenny's cold nose pressed against Lynn's throat. She was sobbing now. Lynn felt the hot moisture of her tears. "Oh, what if we don't find her? What if they do bad things to her?"

"It's okay, honey." Lynn held Jenny tight. "We'll find her. Don't worry. She's going to be all right...." Lynn realized she was murmuring the soothing words to herself as much as to the distraught child.

Ross stood. "You'd better take her inside." He turned to Mrs. Parchly, who wore an expression of horrified disbelief. "Does the school have a nurse?"

Mrs. Parchly didn't answer. She made a low, frightened sound.

Lynn answered for her. "The nurse is only here on Tuesdays and Thursdays."

Ross swore. "See if you can dig up some blankets, okay? Whatever you can find to keep this woman warm until the ambulance comes."

Lynn nodded, her nose brushing the soft little pom-pom at the crown of Jenny's bright pink wool hat. "All right," she said. Her voice sounded calm.

But she didn't feel calm. Inside, she was screaming.

Screaming for Sara, with her fighter's spirit and her unzippable mouth. Sara.

Kidnapped.

By two men in ski masks. Two thugs who thought nothing of roughing up a woman, knocking her unconscious to the ground and then leaving her there.

Oh, God, Lynn's heart cried. Sara! Where are you? Sara, *please* be all right....

Lynn scanned the deserted parking lot, taking in the rows of cars, the silent trees. Steadily the snow came down, like something in a picture postcard, so pretty and white....

"Go on, Lynn," Ross said. "Get the blankets. I'll stay here with the woman."

"Yes." Lynn held the sobbing Jenny closer. "Yes, right away."

They went straight to the office, where Mrs. Parchly broke down. "Oh, this is terrible," she muttered, shaking her head. "What have I done? I should have been watching. I shouldn't have let them out of my sight."

Trish went right to her, led her to the cot in the small nurse's cubicle down the hall. Lynn followed after, gratitude washing through her that Trish was here. Trish might be spoiled and self-absorbed sometimes. But she could be tough, too. She could keep her head in a crisis.

Lynn passed Jenny to Trish as soon as Trish had made the secretary comfortable.

"What in blue blazes is going on?" Trish demanded.

Quickly, Lynn explained the situation.

Trish sank to a chair, cradling Jenny, who by then was crying for her mother. "It's all right, sweetie-pie," Trish crooned. "Shh, it's okay. Your mommy will be here. She'll be here real soon...." She pointed to a cupboard. "The blankets are in there."

Lynn grabbed three of them, as well as a pillow, then whirled for the door again.

"Take my coat," her sister called after her. "It's on that rack right by the door!"

Lynn grabbed the coat, shoved her arms into the too-short sleeves and went out again.

She heard the sirens in the distance just as she reached Ross's side. Together they wrapped the blankets around the still-unconscious woman. Ross lifted her head enough to slide the pillow beneath it. When he pulled his hand away, drying blood clung to his fingers.

"Oh, God…" Lynn whispered as the sirens screamed their way toward them.

Ross sent her a steadying glance. "It felt like only a surface cut. And it's not the blood on the outside that's the problem, anyway."

She nodded. She knew her first aid. It would be the blood caught beneath the skull, causing uncontrollable swelling, that could end this woman's life.

"What's happening here?" Lynn looked up. The principal, Mrs. Taggert, was standing over them. Trish must have alerted her. She knelt beside them. "Mrs. Sheppard…dear God."

Ross looked up. "Your secretary says she's a teacher."

"Yes. Mrs. Angela Sheppard. She just left my office, not ten minutes ago." Mrs. Taggert glanced toward the entrance to the parking lot. "There's the ambulance. Good."

The white van, lights flashing, came toward them. The sheriff's department SUV was right behind it.

They took Angela Sheppard, who remained unconscious, to Whitehorn Memorial Hospital.

Recently elected sheriff Rafe Rawlings collected statements from everyone. In the meantime, his partner, a new deputy, Shane McBride, secured the parking lot and then scoured the area for signs of the two masked men and the stolen child. Shane didn't find much, but he did discover Angela Sheppard's purse, under the car, right near where she had fallen.

Danielle and Jessica McCallum arrived to pick up

their daughters before Rafe and Shane had finished their work.

Lynn would never forget the look of utter desolation on her dear friend's face when they told her that her child was missing. Danielle remained calm throughout. A deadly, terrifying kind of calm. Sterling McCallum, Jenny's adoptive father and a special investigator in the sheriff's office, appeared a few minutes later. After a quick session with the sheriff, the deputy, the principal and Ross, where the others brought him up to speed on the situation, he insisted that Danielle go home with Jessica and Jenny.

At two-thirty, Ross left to return to his office.

He took Lynn aside before he went.

"Are you all right?" he asked softly.

She nodded.

"I've got appointments at three and four o'clock, but I'll come to your house as soon as I can get away."

She only stared at him, wondering what that meant, if he was putting out some hope for the two of them now—or if he just wanted to be certain that she was keeping it together, that emotionally she was managing to deal with the horror of Sara's disappearance.

He peered at her more closely. "You're *sure* you're okay?"

"I am fine."

"All right, then." And he was gone.

A few minutes later Lynn volunteered to take the prostrate Mrs. Parchly home. She stayed there with the secretary until Mr. Parchly arrived at four. Then Lynn drove to the McCallums' house, where for two hours she sat at the kitchen table with Danielle. Jessica made sandwiches. Lynn ate hers by rote, hardly tasting it, worried sick about Sara, hoping Jenny would come through this all right.

Jenny's pediatrician, Carey Hall Kincaid, had already dropped by to see the child. Now Jenny was resting in her room, her dog Sugar in bed with her, a special treat, which Jessica had allowed because of the circumstances.

They went over the few facts that the sheriff and the deputy had discovered. Jessica added that Rafe Rawlings and Shane McBride had already begun gathering what information they could on the history of Angela Sheppard. Maybe something in the woman's past would tell them why two thugs in ski masks might have been after her. Better yet, perhaps she'd regain consciousness soon and tell them herself.

Carefully they all avoided speculation about where Sara might be right now, though Lynn felt certain the scary subject was foremost in each of their minds.

Danielle grew somewhat agitated as the time crawled by. She wanted to be at home, she said. Maybe, somehow, Sara or the men who had taken her would try to reach her there. Jessica reminded her that Rafe Rawlings did have a deputy stationed at her house, that the man could handle anything that happened there. But Danielle said she needed to be there, just in case; she had to be the one to answer if an important call did come in.

Sterling came home at five minutes of six. He had no news, but asked Danielle if she had a recent picture of Sara. They would put it on a flyer and run off several thousand. Then tomorrow they could start calling around, asking everyone they knew to come in and pick up a stack of the things, to plaster all over every available bulletin board and telephone pole for miles around.

Danielle stood. "I have her school picture. At my house—which is where I'm going now."

"I really wish you'd stay with us," Jessica suggested one more time.

But Sterling said, "She's right. If a call does come in, she should be there to answer it."

Danielle spoke to Sterling again. "If you'll follow me over there, I'll give you the picture."

Lynn offered to go along, to stay with her for the night.

Danielle shook her head. "Go on home now. I'll have the deputy there with me, if I need anyone."

"But—"

"Lynn. I'm all right. And I'm used to handling things on my own."

Lynn looked at her friend's pale, sct face and wondered about Danielle's husband. Where was the man? Would Danielle try to reach him, now that their child was missing?

Lynn wanted to ask. But she feared that such questions would only dredge up more misery.

"You'll call me. If there's anything…?"

"You know I will."

Lynn got into her Blazer and went home. The snow had stopped by then, leaving a few inches of crystalline whiteness layering the yards of the houses she passed, and piled along the curbs in muddy mounds.

At home she found Ross's Mercedes parked in

front of the house—and Trish's little compact waiting in the driveway.

She discovered them both sitting in the living room. Neither looked overjoyed at the presence of the other.

Trish announced sourly, "He said you were expecting him. So I went ahead and let him in." She stood. "Where were you?"

"At the McCallums' house. With Danielle."

"Danielle. That poor woman. How is she?"

"She's holding up incredibly well. Considering."

"Thank the Lord for small favors," Trish declared. She cast a sideways glance at Ross, then spoke to Lynn again. "Walk me to the door?"

"Trish. You don't have to leave."

Trish only waved a hand at that remark. Lynn followed her to the entrance hall, where Trish leaned close and spoke in a whisper, for Lynn's ears alone. "You're still in love with him. I know that. And you know what? I think he's just crazy over you. I think you better take him back."

Lynn made a face at her sister and pitched her voice equally low. "A few days ago, you said you hated him."

Trish shrugged and leaned close again. "He's not my favorite person in the world, I admit it. But hey. If you love him, well, you're my sis and I want you to have him."

Lynn wished it could be that simple.

Trish seemed to think that it was. "Sometimes, Lynnie, the best way to get what you want is to just go ahead and go after it, you know?"

It was Lynn's turn to shrug. She touched her sister's shoulder fondly. "I was so grateful today, that you were there."

Now Trish was grinning. "Kept my head pretty good, didn't I?"

"You were terrific."

"That poor little Sara. Lord, I hope she's all right. How's Mrs. Parchly?"

"She'll get through it. We all will. Somehow."

"Amen to that." Trish pulled open the door and paused on the threshold, where she whispered some more. "I mean it. You want that man, you take him. He's a goner. I can see it when he looks at you." Her green eyes gleamed. "And he does have all that nice money, you know. Now, I'm not saying a girl should marry a man for his money. But all in all, I personally would rather be rich."

"Get out of here."

With a wink and a chuckle, Trish went on her way.

Lynn took a minute, standing there in the front hall, to gather her nerve. Then she marched back into the living room, where Ross was waiting.

He'd left his seat at the end of the sofa and wandered over to the old upright piano in the corner. He was studying the cluster of family photographs arranged in a variety of ornate frames on the high-backed lid.

Lynn drew to a halt several feet from him.

He turned to her, and she saw the yearning in his eyes. Her heart rose. Yes, she thought. Say it, Ross. Oh, please, say the words....

But then he only gestured at the photographs. "Your father was a handsome man."

She contained her disappointment and answered him in kind. "Yes. And a good man, too."

"Blue eyes. Like yours."

"That's right."

"This piano…?"

"My mother's."

"Do you play?"

"Not as well as my mother did, but I have been known to pound out a tune or two now and then."

A silence fell. He seemed not to know what to say next.

So she went ahead and challenged, "What is it, Ross? Why are you here?"

He answered too quickly. "I was worried about you."

"Well, I'm just fine. You can see that."

He looked doubtful—or maybe it was only that he didn't want to believe her. If he believed her, then to his mind he'd have no reason to linger.

"You've returned my shoe—or at least, I know where it is now." On the floor of her classroom. Where she'd dropped it when she threw herself into his arms. "And I've just told you, for about the tenth time, that I am fine. There's no real reason for you to stay. Unless you *want* to stay."

He took a long time to reply. And when he did, his voice was harsh and low. "Damn it. You know what I want."

"Well, then, why don't you just reach out and take it?"

He closed his eyes, turned his head away.

"Ross. Please…" She took a step toward him.

"No," he said. "You can do better than someone like me."

"Oh, Ross. If you'll only—"

He silenced her by raising his hand. "I'd better go now."

"I'm not *asking* you to go."

But he wasn't listening. He muttered, "Good night, Lynn." Then he strode around her and right on out the front door.

She gave him ten minutes. Then she went after him.

Chapter Seventeen

Twenty-six minutes later, she was knocking at his door.

It took him about three more minutes to answer. She forgave him for that. After all, it was a big house.

"What in hell are you doing here?" he growled when he finally opened the door.

"Lovely to see you, too." And it was, actually. He had switched his boots for moccasins and traded his fine sweater and slacks for a pair of faded jeans and a gray sweatshirt. "You look comfortable."

"I was getting there."

"Past tense. You mean, the sight of me has made you *un*comfortable?"

"What do you want, Lynn?"

"I believe we've been through all that. May I come in?"

He didn't budge.

Maybe he needed to hear a few cold, hard facts. She decided to provide them.

"Ross. There is a child I love out there somewhere in this cold winter night. She could be hurt. She could be—God forgive me for saying it—she could be dead. If she's alive, I know she is terrified. Every time I think of her, I want to scream. I want to tear out my hair. And I want to do what you did when you found out your wife was cheating on you. That is to say, I want to throw up."

He was glowering at her. Lynn didn't let that stop her. "In addition to that lost child, there is a woman alone, without that child, *her* child. And without her husband. With only a sheriff's deputy and a telephone—a telephone that most likely is not ringing—to keep her company tonight."

A gust of icy wind blew across the wide front deck. Lynn shivered, pulled her coat closer around her. "I told you I was fine. Well, compared to that child and that woman, I am. And I have been thinking. Sara is alone, except for the cold-blooded monsters who took her. And Danielle is alone—because, she said, she's used to being that way. But I don't want to be alone, Ross. I want to be with you."

Lord, it did look as if, just maybe, she had gotten through to him. He wasn't scowling anymore.

He asked, very quietly, "Are you sure?"

"Yes, I am. Now, would you please let me in? It's cold out here."

He moved aside. She went straight to the coat closet and hung up her coat. She dropped her purse on the floor. Then she shut the closet door.

He was leaning against the stair rail, arms crossed over his broad chest, watching her.

First things first, she thought. "Did you eat anything?"

"Since when?"

"Oh, let's see. In the past six hours or so?"

"No."

"Then let's go into the kitchen and see what we can find."

Twenty minutes later, she slid a mushroom omelet, a big glass of milk and a stack of toast onto the table. She pulled out the nearest chair. "Sit down, please, and eat."

He grunted in annoyance, but he did sit down. Then he looked up at her skeptically. "What about you?"

"I had a sandwich at Jessica's. I'm fine." She slid in across from him. "Eat."

He picked up his fork and dug in.

She leaned her elbows on the table and watched him. "You *were* hungry."

"Is that an accusation?"

"Not at all."

She watched him some more. He took a bite, swallowed some milk, then set the glass down. "All right. Whatever's going on in that mind of yours, tell me."

She confessed, "I do want to talk to you...."

"About what?"

About you and me, she thought. About how I love you—and my baby sister says that you love me.

But they would get to that. Right now, there was something else, something she really had to share with someone. And who better than the man she loved? "I've been thinking."

He shoveled in another bite of egg, made a questioning sound.

"I never told you this. It just felt too embarrassing, because of our circumstances. But remember that morning, the morning after our…one night together?"

Good thing she wasn't standing; the look that he sent her would have buckled her knees. "I remember."

"I told you that Winona Cobbs picked me up."

"So?"

"Well, when she drove up and found me, at the end of your drive out there, she had…a vision, I guess you could call it."

He raised a dark brow. "A vision." The flat way he said that told her exactly what he thought of such things.

"Hear me out. Please."

He studied her for a moment, then shrugged. "Go ahead."

"They do say that Winona has the sight. She's predicted more than one disaster around these parts—and she's also seen what would happen, how things would work out in the end. Sometimes they even consult her, at the sheriff's office, when—"

"I get the point. Get back to that morning."

"Yes. All right. She took my red shoe and she—"

"Wait a minute. Your *shoe?*"

"Yes. I was carrying it, since I couldn't find the other one. And she reached out the window of her pickup and took it. She…held it to her chest and she started rocking in her seat, making this humming sound. And then she kind of…chanted. She chanted strange things."

He demanded, "What things?"

The clock on the mantel chimed. One stroke. Seven-thirty. Lynn closed her eyes, trying to call it all up, the chilly October morning, herself, her feet cut and aching. And Winona, rocking. Chanting…

"She said, 'What is lost shall be found, in a scattering of dust.'" Lynn opened her eyes, looked at Ross expectantly.

He didn't seem terribly impressed. "And just what should I make of that?"

She blew out a frustrated breath. "My red shoe, that's what."

"Lynn…"

"No. I mean it. Think about it. My shoe was lost—and then found, 'in a scattering of dust.' Get it? Your new housekeeper. Dusting."

His lips flattened out—but at least he restrained himself from rolling his eyes. "What else did Winona say during this *vision* of hers?"

"She said…'a ring and a lie'—that the lie would bring truth. She said something about 'them' taking the wrong twin. And that love would return, in…a dark night of fear and misery. She said, 'The teacher teaches, the prince must learn,' and—"

"Oh, come on. She said that, about the ring? About a teacher, and a prince?"

"I swear to you. She said it."

"I don't believe—"

"I know you don't." She didn't let her gaze waver. "And that's the problem—*our* problem, anyway. Isn't it? That you don't believe. That you'll let what went wrong in the past keep you from hoping…from *loving,* right now?"

The look he gave her then made her want to leap from her chair and throw herself into his arms.

She stayed where she was. He pushed his plate away. "Go on. Tell me the rest."

"All right. There was...something about silence. That there would be silence, a *horrible* silence, when the 'lost one' came back...."

He stared at her, his jaw set—and his eyes full of doubts.

She wanted to reach out and shake him. "Oh, Ross. Don't you see? The way Jenny and Sara are. Like sisters. Like...twins. And Winona said they would take the 'wrong' twin. Could that mean they were supposed to take Jenny, somehow, do you think? And Winona did say *when*—when the lost one came back. That means Sara will be returned to us, don't you think?"

"I don't know *what* to think. What else did she say?"

"Only one more thing. That...love was magic. That I should believe in it and it wouldn't let me down."

He waited, as if he expected her to say something more. When she didn't, he prompted, "That's all?"

"Yes," she replied, irritation making the word curt. "And I think it's plenty." She stood. "I should have thought about this, *really* thought about it, earlier. I should have realized—"

"What? What's to realize?"

She experienced the urge to shake him again. "How can you say that, after what I just told you?"

"Lynn, listen. Yes, it does make a strange kind of sense. But are there any real *clues* there, anything solid that would help us find Sara? I'm sorry, but I don't think so. What you have are predictions, that's all. They don't *lead* anywhere.''

''But—''

''Look. Do you want to call Sterling?''

''Yes. Yes, I do.''

''Then the phone's over there, and the phone book's in the top drawer, under the bar.''

Lynn got the number and called the McCallums' house as Ross cleared off his place and put his dishes in the dishwasher.

When she hung up, he was waiting, standing on the other side of the table from her. ''Well?''

She wrapped her arms around her middle and slumped against the wall. ''Sterling said he'd get one of the deputies to track down Winona right away. He said that at this point, anything was worth a shot.''

His dark eyes were soft right then. ''You don't look too happy.''

''Sterling reacted the same way you did. He said that he couldn't see anything really solid there, that it was all pretty vague.'' She put both hands against her mouth, then dropped them to her sides. ''Oh, Ross. I just can't stop thinking of her…of Sara…out there in the dark somewhere, with those two awful men.…''

''Hey.'' In five long strides he was around the table and at her side.

''I just…I keep thinking, you know? Keep thinking, What if? What if I'd walked the girls to the multipurpose room myself? Or what if they'd gone five minutes earlier? Or five minutes later? What if—''

He put a finger to her lips and spoke so tenderly. ''What ifs won't help. Take my word for it. I know.''

She captured his hand, held it tightly—to her heart.

And he said, "I've been through all the what ifs myself. Over Elana. What if I hadn't said all those ugly things, what if I'd tried to understand, what if I'd opened my damn eyes earlier, back when we were first starting out? What if I'd let myself see that she loved me and needed me and didn't know how to get through to me? What if. What if? It goes around and around. And it also goes nowhere."

She swallowed. "You have to…let it go."

"I know. And so do you."

"But I want to *help*. I want to *do* something."

"You've done everything you can."

"It's not enough. There has to be more."

"Lynn. Listen. You've done a number of things I would have called impossible. You've made peace with that exasperating family of yours. You've found your sister a job that it appears she's actually going to be good at. You've made a man like me start thinking that maybe there's some kind of hope for him, after all."

"I…I have?"

"You have. But with this. With Sara's disappearance. There is no more you can do. You're going to have to put a little faith in Rafe and Sterling and the deputies."

"But I—"

He shook his head. "No more buts."

She stared at him, knowing he was right, and still wishing with all of her heart that he wasn't—at least not about Sara.

And then she couldn't stand it anymore. She let her body sway toward him.

Those strong arms went around her. She sighed,

rested against him. He stroked her hair, cradled her head in the crook of his shoulder. She thought, yes…oh, yes. This is where I was meant to be. Here. In this man's arms.

She looked up at him.

"Better?" he asked.

"A little."

He traced her brows with a finger, then guided a stray curl off her cheek. "You've done what you could."

"It's not much."

"We'll call. In the morning. See what they found out."

We, she thought. *We'll call.* That did sound good.

He was smiling. Lord, how she loved that smile of his. "Okay. You've fed me. You've called Sterling and told him all about Winona's predictions. Now what?"

The clock on the mantel chimed the hour then. "Eight o'clock," she whispered. His lips were so close. She brushed a kiss across them.

His arms tightened around her. He asked again, very low this time, "Now what?"

And she said, "Now, Mr. Garrison, I take you to bed."

Chapter Eighteen

Deep in the night, she woke with a cry.

Ross reached for her. Downstairs, the clock struck two.

"Bad dream?" He held her close.

She dragged in a shuddery breath and nodded against his chest. "About Sara. She was calling me. I couldn't find her. And then...we were in my classroom. She said, 'You forgot my puppy, Miss Taylor. You know that you did.'"

His lips brushed her hair. "What puppy?"

She put her hand on his chest. She loved that, the feel of him against her fingertips. "Sara told me a few months ago...it was my birthday, as a matter of fact, right before you came in the door. Remember?"

She felt his nod. "That's right. Sara was there with you that day."

"She was...teasing me, really. About how she

couldn't tell me what my birthday present would be. She's just such a talker. She'll get going and you can't get her to stop. We used to have a signal. I would pretend I was pulling a zipper across my lips. And she would giggle and say, 'I know. Zipper my lip....' Oh, Ross..."

"It's all right," he murmured. "Come on, now. It's all right..."

She lifted her hand from his chest and brushed the tears away. "I...about the puppy..."

"I'm listening."

She laid her hand on his chest again. It felt so right there, against his warmth and his strength. Lightly, she rubbed. The crisp hair felt silky, so alive, so very real.

"The puppy," he reminded her.

"Yes. The puppy." A wobbly little smile came. She felt it, tugging at the edges of her mouth. "It was my birthday. And we were waiting for Danielle to come. And Sara got to rambling, about Christmas, and how she wanted a puppy. A puppy that would grow up to be like Jenny's dog, Sugar. Sara said she really, really wanted that. I made a mental note to mention it to Danielle. But somehow..."

He knew what she was going to say. "You never got around to it."

She lifted herself up, so she could see him. The room was dim, the one light on the nightstand turned down low. But his eyes were clear to her, and that was all that mattered. "Oh, Ross. I just keep thinking, what if she never gets her puppy, never sings her little duet with Jenny at the Christmas pageant, never even *has* another Christmas? What if she's—?"

"Shh," he said. "No what ifs, remember?"

"Yes. Yes, I know you're right...."

He kissed her, a tender, seeking kiss, slowly pushing her back into the pillows as he did it, curving his body over hers. Then he lifted his mouth, just a fraction.

He spoke against her lips. "She'll come back. Remember? Your town psychic said so."

"But *you* said—"

"What the hell do I know? I'm only a man."

"But—"

"Don't argue. Just believe."

The tears rose again. Was she dreaming? Or had Ross Garrison just told *her* to believe?

"Do it," he commanded. Then he said it a second time. "Believe."

"I—"

He kissed her again, and she forgot how to speak.

She forgot everything but his mouth on hers, his hands roaming her body, tender and insistent, finding all her secret places and opening them, arousing them.

His mouth followed his hands, downward.

She clutched his dark head as his mouth found her. She felt his tongue, stroking her, bringing stars and moons to spin behind her eyelids, until she rolled her head on the pillow and cried out, lost to all but the fulfillment pulsing and shimmering out from his stroking tongue to every nerve she possessed.

A few minutes later she helped him with the little foil packet, removing the condom and sliding it down over the thick length of him.

He guided her to the top position. She rode him,

looking down into his face, thinking, I love you.... And yes. Oh, yes...I will believe....

He surged up into her. She took him deep. They cried out as one. The clock struck the half hour. They smiled at each other. And then they settled back down to steal a few hours of sleep.

The clock was just striking nine when the phone rang. Lynn woke to a moment of panic, thinking she had to get to school, that her students would all be there, waiting, wondering where their teacher was.

But then she remembered. Today was Saturday.

Saturday. No school.

And Sara was missing....

Ross reached over and snatched the phone from the nightstand. "Garrison here."

Lynn heard the murmur of a voice at the other end of the line.

Then Ross asked, "Half an hour ago?"

"Is it Sterling?" she whispered.

He held up a hand to silence her, then gave her a nod. "All right," he said into the phone. "Yes. Ten-thirty. My office."

"Ask him about Winona. Did they talk to her?"

He patted the air for silence, listened to Sterling some more. Then he muttered more agreements, said, "We'll see what we can do. What about the Sheppard woman? Anything there?"

She heard Sterling start talking again, and couldn't stop herself from urging, "Ross. Please. Winona..."

Another curt nod, then, "Sterling. By the way, did you talk to the Cobbs woman?...Yes. I know Lynn called you...Yes. All right. I understand. And I'll see you at ten-thirty...."

He dropped the phone back in its cradle.

"What?" she demanded, dragging herself up against the headboard. "What's happened?"

He sat up, too. "They got a ransom demand. At eight-thirty this morning. A call from a pay phone. They couldn't trace it, damn it. They didn't even have a chance to try. The call came to Sterling's house."

"*Sterling's* house?"

"That's what I said. They had no equipment set up there. They thought, if anything, the call would come at Danielle's. They were ready there. But no such luck."

"The demand...what was it?"

"A million dollars."

"Oh, my Lord."

"A million dollars," Ross repeated. "For the return of Jennifer McCallum."

Lynn gasped. "*Jenny?* But—" Understanding dawned. "Wait a minute. The coats...Jenny and Sara switched coats. Jenny's name is sewn inside her collar. Those horrible men must think—"

"Yeah. They think they've got Jennifer. And apparently they know about the Kincaid fortune."

"Ross. It's coming out as Winona predicted. Remember what she said. 'They will take the wrong twin....'"

He swore. "It does look that way, doesn't it?"

"But wouldn't Sara have told them—" A small cry escaped her. "Oh, Ross. Why didn't she tell them? Unless she's—"

"Don't jump to conclusions," he ordered gruffly. "It's possible they didn't give her a chance to tell them. Or she could be keeping her mouth shut."

Lynn closed her eyes, let out a moan. "But Sara never keeps her mouth shut."

"Remember. She's got to be scared out of her wits. Terror can be a real silencer."

"Yes. Oh, yes. That's possible, isn't it?" Lord, she thought, look where we are. To the point where we're hoping Sara is terrified.

Appalling. Sick. To wish terror on a five-year-old.

But Lynn did wish it. If it increased the chances that Sara would come back to them alive.

"We're going to play along," Ross said. "They haven't put out those flyers yet with Sara's picture on them. Now they won't put them out. We'll try to contain it, talk to everyone who knows the facts and insist that they keep their mouths shut."

She thought of Winona again. And of Lily Mae, Winona's dearest friend. And Mrs. Parchly. And her own sister. All of them loved nothing so much as to share what they knew. "Half the town has to know by now."

"We'll do all we can."

"Yes. Yes, of course. What about the ransom?"

"We're going to pay it."

"How?"

He was already pushing the covers back. "Look, I've got to get moving. I'll tell you everything. Later."

"But what about the woman? What about Angela Sheppard?"

He swung his feet to the rug and then paused to look back at her. "She regained consciousness last night. Shane McBride interviewed her. He got nothing. Apparently the blow to her head has affected her short-term memory. She doesn't seem to have a clue what's going on—and I do have to get going.'' He leaned back, canted toward her and pressed a quick, savage kiss on her mouth. ''I need to get to my office, go over the Kincaid Trust documents. We've got a meeting about this in an hour and a half.'' He slid away and stood.

Lynn leaned across the bed and grabbed his hand. ''One more thing. Winona?''

He gave a single shake of his head. ''Nothing. Sherrif Rawlings talked to her. She said she wasn't 'getting anything' on the situation, but that she would contact him immediately if anything came to her.''

She released him with a sigh. ''That's…disappointing.''

He said nothing. He was already striding toward the bathroom, heading for a shower.

Lynn sat there in the tangled bed for a moment, her shoulders slumped, wondering what the world was coming to.

But then she ordered some starch into her sagging backbone and jumped from the bed. She gathered up her clothes and put them on, then ran downstairs to get the coffee going.

Ross kissed her goodbye at nine-forty.

She pressed herself against him and put her whole heart in that kiss.

''Call me,'' she begged. ''After the meeting…''

He said that he would. Then he got into his Mercedes and she climbed into her Blazer. She followed him down the long driveway.

He left her behind when they got to town. He turned for his office and she turned for her house.

At home she showered, then made some calls. To Trish and then to Mrs. Parchly, letting them know of the new developments, warning them not to tell other people that it was Sara and not Jenny the two thugs had kidnapped.

Then she waited. The minutes seemed like centuries.

Finally, at eleven-thirty, the phone rang.

It was Ross, calling as he'd promised he would to report on the meeting he'd just had with Sterling.

He said what she already knew. There was no way that Danielle could come up with a million dollars in the next day or two. So Sterling and Jessica had decided they wanted the Kincaid Trust to pay the ransom. Ross had studied the terms of the trust. It was stretching it a little, but he was making arrangements to free up the money.

He also said the McCallums were worried for Jenny, that she might still be in danger should the kidnappers learn they'd taken the wrong child. Arrangements had been made for Jenny to stay someplace safe for a while. Ross said he couldn't tell her where. The fewer people who knew, the better for everyone.

Lynn had to agree. "Now what?" she asked.

"Now we wait," he said. "The kidnappers said they'd call soon with further instructions."

He said goodbye right after that. Lynn stood by the phone, feeling useless and frustrated.

There had to be *something* that she could do.

The idea came to her like the proverbial bolt out of the blue.

Was it crazy?

Maybe.

Silly?

Perhaps a little.

But, as Sterling McCallum had said last night, at this point, anything was worth a shot.

She looked up Winona's number. The woman took six rings to answer the phone. Lynn chewed her lip and waited.

Finally she heard the psychic's voice. "Winona's Stop 'n Swap. One man's trash is another man's treasure."

Lynn said hello—and then made her request.

Winona hedged a little. "Child, the spirits are not a radio program. You can't just…flip a dial and expect to tune in."

"Please, Winona. Won't you please try?"

Winona sighed and agreed that she would.

"Would you like me to come out there, to the Stop 'n Swap?"

"No, dear. I'll come to you."

"When?"

"An hour?"

"I'll be waiting."

Exactly sixty minutes later, Lynn opened the door to admit the psychic—and Lily Mae Wheeler, as well.

"I hope you don't mind, honey." Bracelets ajingle, Lily Mae patted her hair, which was now blond. "I just happened to be out there at Winona's when you called, looking over some earrings she found in a cigar box. I had to come along."

They settled in the living room. Lynn had her red shoe ready. She handed it to Winona.

Winona went through the motions, holding the shoe to her breast, closing her eyes, rocking back and forth.

Lynn and Lily Mae waited, still as statues, afraid

to move lest they disturb whatever currents of psychic energy Winona might be trying to receive.

Finally Winona's eyes popped open. She let out a gusty breath. "I'm sorry. There's nothing. Just nothing at all." She looked down at the shoe. "It's just a shoe to me now. And hugging it feels...pretty darn foolish, I must say."

Lynn had that urge again: to scream. To tear her hair. She jumped to her feet. "Maybe some tea, do you think? I have Oolong, and herbal tea. We could...draw all the curtains. And...candles. Yes. I have candles, in the kitchen drawer, for when the power goes out. We could—"

"Honey." Lily Mae was shaking her blond head. "You've got to settle down...."

"No. No, this will work. It *has* to work. Just...stay there. I think we can skip the tea. But the curtains. And the candles. I'm sure they will help."

The two older women shook their heads. Lynn ignored them. She flew to the kitchen drawer, got the votive candles in their little jars, and the matches as well. When she returned to the living room, Lily Mae was already up, drawing the curtains.

Lynn lined up the candles on the coffee table. "There are six of them. Is six a good number?"

"Child..." Winona clucked her tongue sadly.

"Well, six is what I've got. It's going to have to do." Lynn lighted the candles. Then she and Lily Mae sat down again.

Winona hugged the red shoe some more.

But it was no good.

"I'm sorry," the psychic said. "So sorry, about this—"

"Wait." Lynn jumped up again. "Please. Stay

right there. Don't go anywhere. I'll be back in twenty minutes, I promise you.'' She scooped her purse from an end table and raced for the door.

She drove straight to the school, left her Blazer running in the bus lane and dashed to her classroom.

The shopping bag was waiting, on her desk, where the janitor must have set it when he was cleaning the room. She grabbed it and ran out again.

''Oh, no,'' she muttered to herself when she swung back into her driveway. ''Ross.''

The black Mercedes SUV gleamed in the afternoon sun, right there at her curb.

She didn't need his presence right now. She loved him with all that was in her to love, but, oh, not right now. Right now she simply couldn't afford to see the skepticism in those beautiful dark eyes.

With a tiny, distressed moan, she scooped up the bag and leaned on her door handle.

They were all there, in the living room. Lily Mae and Winona. And Ross.

And they all shook their heads at her when she walked in.

She glared at Ross. ''If you stay, you had better not say a word.''

Lily Mae actually chuckled. ''I think she means it.''

He sucked in a breath, then nodded.

''Not a peep,'' Lynn insisted.

He nodded again.

''Fine, then. Sit over there.''

He dropped to the free end of the sofa, down from Lily Mae.

Lynn took the second red shoe from the bag. ''Winona, this is the shoe that was missing, that morning when you picked me up. I thought—''

''I understand, child. Sit down.'' Lynn took the vacant chair. ''Now.'' Winona snapped her fingers. ''The shoe.''

Her heart pounding triple time, Lynn handed it over.

Winona clutched the shoe close. ''Hmm,'' she said. ''Hmmmmm...'' The wrinkled eyelids drooped shut. She rocked back and forth.

On the table before them the candle flames rose up, shrank down, and then rose up again, higher than before.

Joy surged through Lynn, hot and bright, fierce and triumphant. It was happening. It was working....

That humming sound went on, seeming to come from Winona but not from Winona. Sounding like the pines in the wind, like a song remembered, but not quite known.

Lynn waited, perched there on the edge of her chair—she waited for the words. The words that would tell her, would tell all of them, where to find Sara.

Finally the words came.

''Babies. Two babies. A woman starting over and the little bird who sings. A man who seeks the lost one...a man of healing hands. A child returned. In silence, holly in her hair. And a father...a father returning, as well. A father seeking answers. Seeking truth. And finding...love. The love he thought lost to him. The love that still lives...in the heart of a woman, who waits now, but not for him...'' Winona's eyelids fluttered open. She turned her head, looked at Lynn, looked *through* Lynn. The candle flames gleamed in those fathomless eyes, pinpoints of golden light.

"Trust," Winona chanted. "Believe. Wait. All will be answered. Take this love that is given you, diamond-bright. For it *is* magic. The only true magic we have in this world…"

Winona sighed. Her eyelids fluttered down again. The candle flames flickered. Then, as one, they went out.

Winona said in a clear, very alert-sounding voice, "Open the curtains, child. It's too dark in here."

"Stay put, honey," said Lily Mae. She popped up in a jingling of jewelry and drew back the drapes.

Lynn leaned toward Winona. "But…what did it *mean?*"

Winona was smiling, a bright, wide-awake smile. "If I knew that, I'd know everything, wouldn't I?"

"Oh, I should have taped it, shouldn't I? How will we remember it all, to tell Sterling and Rafe?"

"Don't worry," said Winona. She tapped a finger to her temple. "I have it all. Right here. It's still quite clear. Every word of it. It's usually like that, for an hour or two after the event."

"You have to talk to—"

"Yes. I know." Winona stood. "Come along, Lily Mae. We must pay a visit to the sheriff's office right away."

Moments later, only Ross and Lynn remained in the living room, with the winter sun streaming in through the front windows and the faint smell of candle smoke hanging in the air. Lynn's two red shoes stood near the candles, side by side. A matched pair again, at last.

Ross spoke softly. "Believe," he said. "And trust."

She nodded. "I heard her. I truly did. And she did say again that Sara would be returned, didn't she? Oh, Ross. Tell me that was what she said."

He stood. "Yes. She did say it."

In her heart, Winona's chant echoed. *A child returned. In silence, holly in her hair…*

Ross said, "I love you, Lynn."

There it was. Joy. Moving through her once more, banishing all doubt. "I'm so glad."

"I want it settled between us. I was sitting in my office, working over the Kincaid Trust, and it suddenly occurred to me that I had something to do that just couldn't wait. I had to go back to my house. And get this." He reached into the pocket of his beautiful brown cashmere jacket and pulled out the small black velvet case.

Lynn stared at it, cradled there in his tanned hand. *A ring and a lie,* she thought, *A lie that brings truth…*

"Give me your hand."

She closed the distance between them. He opened the case, took out that big two-carat diamond he'd insisted they buy. He set the little box on the coffee table. Then he slid the diamond onto her hand.

"I said I didn't know what love was." His deep voice caught. He swallowed, then went on. "And I didn't. Until you. Please. Wear this ring. Wear it for real. And forever…"

She touched his face.

He asked, "Will you marry me?"

"Yes. Yes, I will.…"

He frowned. "There's something else. Tell me."

"I...want to wait, until Sara comes back to us. Is that all right? Will you do that for me?"

He reached for her. She went into his arms. "Yes," he said in a husky whisper. "I'll wait. I'll wait, if you'll make me a promise."

"Anything."

"I want you to promise me that you won't lose heart, about Sara. That you will trust and have faith that she'll be all right. I want you to promise that you will—"

She knew his next word. They said it together. "Believe."

She held him tighter. "I will. I will believe. Oh, Ross. I love you so."

He tipped her chin up and kissed her, a long, tender kiss, a kiss that warmed her whole body and set her heart on fire.

Magic, thought Lynn. Oh, Winona. You were so right. Through it all, there really is only one magic.

And that is the magic of love.

* * * * *

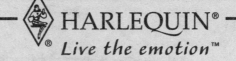

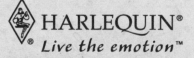

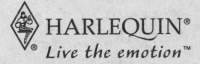

HARLEQUIN®
INTRIGUE®

BREATHTAKING ROMANTIC SUSPENSE

Shared dangers and passions lead to electrifying
romance and heart-stopping suspense!

Every month, you'll meet six new heroes
who are guaranteed to make your spine tingle
and your pulse pound. With them you'll enter
into the exciting world of Harlequin Intrigue—
where your life is on the line
and so is your heart!

THAT'S INTRIGUE—
ROMANTIC SUSPENSE
AT ITS BEST!

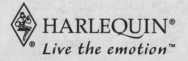

HARLEQUIN®
Live the emotion™

www.eHarlequin.com   INTDIR06

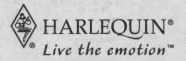

 Harlequin® Historical
Historical Romantic Adventure!

*Imagine a time of chivalrous
knights and unconventional ladies,
roguish rakes and impetuous
heiresses, rugged cowboys
and spirited frontierswomen—
these rich and vivid tales will
capture your imagination!*

*Harlequin Historical . . .
they're too good to miss!*

HHDIR06

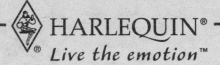